DEATH ON THE THAMES

LONDON COSY MYSTERIES
BOOK 4

RACHEL MCLEAN
MILLIE RAVENSWORTH

ACKROYD
PUBLISHING

Ackroyd Publishing

ackroyd-publishing.com

❁ Created with Vellum

AUTHORS' NOTE

The authors would like to thank the officers of the Marine Policing Unit at Wapping, London, for allowing us to join them for a day and giving us an insight into their vital work and the importance of the Thames to the life of the city. Any mistakes in this book are entirely our fault. Any little dogs on boats in this book are definitely their fault.

CHAPTER ONE

Zaf Williams reckoned he was winning at life.

At times, he was reminded just how lucky he was. And today was one of them. The sun was shining, he'd spent the day showing keen and interested tourists around the beautiful city of London and now he was on his way to meet up with his boyfriend.

He strolled to *Tasty For You*, the café nearest to the bus depot where he worked. He peeked inside the window to catch a glimpse of Alexsei Dadashov at their regular table, the one with the blue chintz tablecloth. After a few moments observing Alexsei unseen he walked in and sat down, smiling. The owner, Levon, had already brought over tea for two in an octagonal steel pot.

"I saw you doing that thing again," said Alexsei. "I pretended not to see."

"Because I'm a weirdo?" asked Zaf.

Alexsei shrugged. "If you like doing it then who am I to spoil your game, eh?"

"You're spoiling it right now." Zaf rolled his eyes. "I just like to count my blessings, that's all."

Alexsei smiled.

"See! You're smiling," said Zaf. "I knew this was a good day."

"You make it sound as if I never smile."

"I never used to see you smiling."

Alexsei had entered Zaf's life as the landlord of his colleague and friend, Diana Bakewell, and had taken a dim view of Zaf seeking refuge in Diana's flat when he'd been homeless. Maybe there was something in Alexsei's brooding looks, that sweep of dark hair and those thick eyebrows, that looked sterner than intended. But now Zaf had learned to see past that to the good-humoured and playful man beneath.

"Maybe now I have something to smile about," said Alexsei. "I don't think that I will ever be as... demonstrative as you are. But I can smile. I am happy."

Zaf grinned. "I am the luckiest man alive."

"Is that so?"

"I was just thinking about how much I love my job, I have an amazing place to live... and I have you."

"You had a good day at work then?"

Zaf had been working as a tour guide for Chartwell and Crouch for less than a year. It didn't pay well, but it was varied and sociable and allowed him to express his fun side. And every day he learned something new.

Zaf nodded. "London is wonderful and strange." He drew an imaginary circle on the table. "One minute, I reckon I know all the roads and the districts and where things are. It's like a big village. Then I get a glimpse into somewhere I never knew about and it blows my mind." He made the circle bigger then smaller. "Is it huge and unknowable, or is it just my own personal stomping ground that I know and love?"

Alexsei shrugged. "It is both."

"It definitely is."

"You should order something to eat," said Alexsei. "I have news."

Zaf looked up in alarm. "Good news or bad news?"

"I don't know."

Zaf picked up the plastic menu. "News that's worthy of cheesy bread?"

Alexsei held up a hand. "Calm yourself, it is only news. Not cheesy bread news, but perhaps egg and chips news."

Zaf ordered the food from Levon and motioned for Alexsei to tell him.

"My father is coming to visit." Alexsei sat back in his seat, the message complete.

"And what does that mean? What's he like?"

Zaf knew almost nothing about Alexsei's dad. Alexsei was Azerbaijani by birth, although had been educated in England and lived most of his life here. Zaf knew that Alexsei's dad, Kamran Dadashov, was a businessman who owned a lot of property, including the huge sub-divided house that Alexsei, Diana and Zaf lived in. Alexsei had the ground floor, Diana the middle flat and Zaf was currently staying in the vacant top floor, at least until it could be properly rented out.

"What's my dad like?" Alexsei's mouth turned up into an almost-smile. "He is *a lot*. When he is in a room, you know he is in the room."

"I need more than that. Are we talking dreadful narcissist, incessant chatterbox or is he, like, seven feet tall?"

"Hey, he's just my dad, I don't know. Well, I do know that

he's not seven feet tall. I guess I'm worried what he might think about us, you know?"

Zaf frowned. "Does he know you're gay?"

Alexsei smirked. "He knows I am gay. But I never had a serious boyfriend, one who would meet him. He will be interested."

"Interested." Somehow Zaf felt like a bug that Kamran Dadashov intended to study under a microscope.

"You can help me, though."

"Gladly."

"He will be here with friends. Rich friends. Super-rich friends. His visits always require lots of planning, and they will need helpers."

"Helpers?"

Alexsei grimaced. "They have this *tradition* and it... it has to be witnessed to be understood. But he would probably like to hire a tour company."

"Oh, no problem," said Zaf, relieved. "Planning is definitely a thing we can help with, whether it's just me or the rest of Chartwell and Crouch."

"Believe me, it is more than one person's work to keep up with the demands of my father and his friends."

"What do we need to do, then?" asked Zaf, his mind already in work mode. If there was a way into his boyfriend's family's good books, then he was keen to get down to business.

"I am not certain what they will do, but I know that they want to start their visit with something impressive."

"Impressive?"

"A statement activity, a grand view. A place to stand and be able to say 'We are here. This is London.'"

"Now *that* is something Chartwell and Crouch can help with."

"And we – they – sorry, my father – didn't give me much notice — they will want it tomorrow."

"We'll get onto it," said Zaf with a nod. "We'll make it a day to remember."

CHAPTER TWO

Tuesday proved to be as sunny and pleasant as Monday.

Diana Bakewell contemplated the light on the red brick buildings of Marylebone as she walked to work. The stereotypical image of London as a grey and rainy city was undeserved. Statistically, it had fewer rainy days than almost anywhere in France, Spain or Italy. But that didn't stop her carrying her duck-headed brolly everywhere she went. Several decades as a tour guide and more than sixty years of living in this city had taught her to be prepared for anything.

The Chartwell and Crouch bus depot was a magical space. To find a covered bus depot of considerable size just off one of London's more crowded streets was to step into a surprisingly spacious and private world. To step through the door-within-a-door for pedestrians, set into the larger door for the buses, was like stepping through a wardrobe into Narnia. Albeit a Narnia full of shiny red London buses.

There was no Aslan in this Narnia, but there was Gus, a big grey tabby cat who was happiest when sprawled out on the seats of one of the vintage Routemaster buses.

Zaf emerged from the office belonging to the depot manager, Paul Kensington. It was a general rule of thumb that they avoided Paul as much as possible.

"Everything okay?" Diana asked.

"Certainly is," Zaf beamed, waggling a bunch of tickets at Diana. "We're off to the London Eye."

She frowned. "What about the Brown family's hundredth birthday party, a tour of the East End where Nana Brown lived during the Blitz?"

Zaf pulled an awkward face. "Yeah. Cancelled. You might want to have a word with Paul about that."

After hearing the rest of the story from Zaf, Diana went into the office. Paul Kensington sat behind his desk tapping at the computer and shaking his head.

"Nana Brown has died?" she said.

Paul glanced up. "It's the worst possible news at the worst possible time."

"You knew the family?"

He blinked. "No, it's the worst news for us, Mrs Bakewell."

Diana ignored the *Mrs*. He should know by now that she had never been married.

"We are living in unprecedented times," he said. "Costs are spiralling out of control and utilisation rates matter."

Diana listened, waiting for him to get to the point.

"If any of our assets achieves less than ninety-five percent utilisation, we're into a loss-making scenario."

"I see," said Diana. "And to be clear, by assets you mean people?"

He gave a dismissive wave. "People, buses... assets. We are faced with upcoming gaps in our schedule, and this is a cause for concern."

"We had a cancellation because our clients suffered a bereavement. The birthday girl herself has passed away."

"Yes."

"But you charged them a cancellation fee anyway to 'balance the books'?" Diana struggled to keep her voice level. That was a client group they were unlikely to see again.

Paul Kensington ignored the question. "Under-utilisation is a matter for every one of us to address, especially those who have contact with service users. Up-sell and cross-sell should always be at the forefront of your mind."

Diana wanted to suggest that giving customers a great experience should be at the forefront of her mind, but she had no desire to prolong the discussion. Her phone buzzed and she pulled it out, relieved.

"Well," she said, "you must be delighted that Zaf has found some fresh customers who want taking on the London Eye."

"It's very much in Zaf's interest to keep our finances afloat," Paul replied. "He's got some expensive training coming up. I've been looking over the curriculum for that GHGC course. We could surely replace some of it with on-the-job training?"

Diana was not going to let Paul cut costs on something as precious as this.

"Respectfully," she said, "I can imagine it might look like that on paper. But when someone's certified as a Guild Heritage Guide, it should help to bring in that extra business we need. It's not only the best possible training, it's also a chance to network with the people that matter across London's heritage sites."

"I'll bear that in mind," said Paul. "Anyway, our fresh customers. I have a contact who's got us some London Eye tickets at a reduced price."

"Sometimes cost is the not the only factor."

He grunted. "You've no head for business, Mrs Bakewell. Too emotional. Were you a hippy in your youth?"

"How old do you think I am?" she replied, and left before he could answer.

Newton Crombie was outside the office, holding a large white cloth and a tin of polish. Newton – driver, engineer, general transportation enthusiast – spent a lot of time and energy on the care of the buses.

"Zaf and I are doing the London Eye this morning," she told him. "Don't think we'll need the bus."

"Can you stick this old shoe in the bin on your way out?" Newton pulled a high-heeled shoe from the pocket of his overall. "Gus brought it in. I think he must have found it in the street."

Diana laughed. "Are you serious? That *old shoe* has a red sole. Is it a Louboutin?"

"What?"

"Christian Louboutin."

Newton peered at it. "Ah. Yes, it does say something like that. Does it belong to this Christian chap, then?"

"It's a designer shoe, Newton. They're five hundred pounds a pair. Gus has very expensive taste." She frowned. "I don't imagine that shoe was discarded in the street. Where did he get it from?"

Right on cue, the cat appeared at Diana's feet with a small chirrup: *fuss, please*. She stooped to tickle under his chin. "Hello, Gus. Whose shoe is that?"

Newton turned it over in his hands. "It looks like a regular shoe to me. I mean, the red sole is a nice detail, but I don't get it."

"Get what?"

"If this is a designer shoe, what makes it more desirable than a cheap shoe?"

Diana tried to think of the best response. "It's not simply about the object itself. It's about the social context and the mystique we associate with the brand. It would be like me asking you why a vintage Routemaster is more desirable than a... what's an example of a modern bus?"

"Something like a Volvo B5LH?"

She nodded. "Why you'd prefer a vintage Routemaster to a Volvo B5LH."

Newton didn't look convinced. Diana held up a hand. "Maybe it's as simple as this. They sold us a story and it's stuck in our collective imaginations. We want to be part of that story. We wear the shoe and we're a certain type of person."

"A wishing shoe?" said Newton with a smile. "Makes sense. I'll put it somewhere safe. Maybe the owner will come looking."

Diana tried to picture a limping woman coming into this place in search of her missing shoe. But stranger things had happened.

CHAPTER THREE

Diana stood with Zaf, looking up at the London Eye.

It had been a short ride of ten stops on the Jubilee Line from Baker Street to Waterloo followed by a stroll to the Jubilee Gardens park on the south bank of the Thames, where the warm weather had brought out the crowds. Jubilee Gardens had a large children's playground, plenty of bench seating and trees for shade. The old London County Hall stood to one side and beyond the gargantuan white structure of the London Eye flowed the Thames itself. The blue-grey waters reflected the sunshine.

"So, clarify this for me again?" she said.

"I've told you everything I know," Zaf replied. "Alexsei's dad is coming with some posh friends and we're showing them the sights of London. And there's something about a *tradition*. I think they meet up a lot."

Diana had only vague recollections of Alexsei's dad. A shape in a doorway, a man in a limo outside the house in Eccleston Square. His visits to London were fleeting, his interests in this country minimal.

And Zaf was nervous, she could tell from the way he was fidgeting and playing with his dark hair.

"I'm sure it'll be marvellous," she said. "We'll need the whole group together, so that we can all be in the same capsule."

"Here they are." Zaf waved as he caught sight of Alexsei emerging from a car on Belvedere Road with two men and a woman.

The family resemblance between Alexsei and his father was obvious. Both had lustrous black hair and deep brown eyes, although Dadashov senior, dressed in a white shirt and casual jacket, had a certain bear-like, husky solidity to him. Diana glanced to her side, where Zaf was watching the newcomers approach. Was he wondering whether Kamran's appearance offered a window into Alexsei's future?

"Morning," said Alexsei. "Here we have Diana and Zaf, who will be assisting us with our needs over the coming days." He gestured towards his companions. "Diana, Zaf, allow me to introduce my father Kamran and his old friend Errol van Blerk. This is Robin Silversmith, who's here to assist."

Errol was a tall, slender man in casual but tailored clothes. Robin wore dark-coloured trousers and a stylish high-necked sweater, a look that would have worked for a gallery owner, the captain of a submarine, or anything in between. She was younger than the men by a good few years.

"Nice to meet you all." Zaf held out his hand.

Kamran looked at the hand as though wondering what to make of it. Robin leaned in and shook it vigorously.

"Good to have a pair of helpers with us," she said. "You have the tickets?"

Zaf brandished the tickets. There were seven tickets, and six of them here. "Are we expecting someone else?"

"Oxnard said he would arrive in his fancy new boat," said Errol. His accent was unmistakeably South African.

"He already *has* a fancy boat," said Kamran. As with his son, there were hints of his Russian-Azeri heritage in his voice, but his English was precise.

"His *new* fancy boat," Errol elaborated, with a smile. "A man is entitled to some small pleasures, eh?"

"Shall we?" said Robin. She gestured towards the London Eye and led the way across the park.

Robin Silversmith seemed to be in charge, despite not being 'one of the boys'. Diana couldn't be sure of her role. Personal assistant? Lawyer? If this Robin was to act as ringmaster of the event, Diana would happily let her assume the role.

Behind her Zaf and Alexsei were talking in low, furtive voices.

"Did I offend your dad or something?" said Zaf.

"Not at all," Alexsei assured him. "You did fine. They have this 'them and us' thing. It's a rich people problem. They'll thaw soon enough."

"Does he have to come by boat?" asked Kamran, walking beside Diana.

"He is keen to show off his yacht," said Errol. "It is a statement, calculated to impress. A big reveal."

"Larger yachts can't come this far up the river, because they won't fit under the bridges," said Diana. "Tower Bridge is the last one they can navigate."

Kamran laughed. "It will be somewhere between a rowing boat and a yacht, then?"

"A Starchaser yacht, I believe," said Robin.

"Here it comes," said Errol.

They leaned against the railings above the Thames,

between the black Victorian lampposts decorated with stylised fish, and watched.

A white boat, more a towering puffed-up speedboat than a yacht in Diana's estimation, swung around in a showy arc in the centre of the river. A suited man waved from the upper deck. The boat moored at a pontoon and the man stepped out onto the pier by County Hall.

"Oxnard Pike. Fashionably late," said Kamran.

Oxnard Pike pulled a pocket watch from his waistcoat pocket. There was something of the academic – or perhaps the Edwardian time traveller – about him.

"Entirely on time," he said. "Did you see my *Silver Salmon*? Makes an impression, doesn't she?"

"More of a minnow, really," replied the South African with a grudging smile.

There were hugs between the three men, accompanied by plenty of hearty backslapping.

"But Mr Dadashov is right," said Robin. "It is time for us to begin. Challenges await."

"Prepare for a thrashing, gents," said Oxnard.

Kamran raised an eyebrow. "You haven't won in four years."

"It's not the winning that's important," said Errol.

Robin turned to Zaf as they approached the queue for the Eye. "Zaf, you have the tickets, I believe. Zaf and Diana are our guides, and along with Alexsei, will be your helpers in the trials to come."

Diana had no idea what any of that meant but didn't let it show. Zaf stepped forward with the tickets.

Time to engage tour guide mode.

"Welcome to the London Eye, everybody," she said, gesturing upwards. "You might think it looks like a really big

Ferris wheel, but it's only supported on one side. As such, it is the world's largest cantilevered observation wheel. There is none taller and the views are spectacular."

Exaggerations weren't needed here. The London Eye, a construction of white tubular metal and polished glass pods, was nothing short of enormous.

"It was opened in the year two thousand to celebrate the millennium," she continued. "If you're all ready, please follow me."

They shuffled into the barricades that funnelled the crowds towards the pods. An assistant scanned their tickets and his machine made an unhappy buzz.

"I'm sorry." The young man looked up at Diana. "These are invalid."

She drew closer, lowering her voice. "Invalid? How is that possible?"

He gave a sympathetic shrug. "Sorry. These aren't from the official website, are they?"

Diana sighed. *Paul Kensington.* If these were pirated tickets...

Diana thought quickly, scanning the crowds.

"Is Heather here?" she asked.

"Heather?"

"Site security. Heather." Diana knew people at all London's landmarks, and this was no exception.

"Sorry, I don't know who that is. You can try buying tickets at the box office, but we're very busy today."

There was no point pressing the matter. Already, their super-slick day for these rich patrons was coming unstuck. Diana had come across concierge agencies that offered services to the ultra-rich. Their requests ranged from shipping cars across the world to emergency bonsai maintenance, and the expectation was that mistakes would not be made.

She turned to the group with a wide smile.

"I forgot that we'd planned a small surprise for you." She spotted Zaf looking at her, puzzled. "A brief photo shoot with our expert photographer, Zaf. He will document your day. Perhaps you'd like to step over there for some clear shots of the four of you together? Five, ten minutes, perhaps?"

She gave Zaf a focused look, hoping he'd pick up on the nature of the emergency.

His eyes widened and a smile broke out. "Yes of course! Ten minutes to get some really fun pictures of you all. I hope you don't mind stepping over this way? The light is a little cleaner."

CHAPTER FOUR

As Zaf led the party away, Diana hurried to the ticket office in the County Hall building, home of the Greater London Council until the government had disbanded it in the nineteen-eighties. Now the building housed a hotel, an aquarium, several tourist attractions and the London Eye gift shop and ticket office.

She groaned inwardly at the queues as she made her way to the back of one.

"Diana? Diana Bakewell?"

Diana suppressed a shudder at the voice and turned.

"Ariadne." She forced a smile.

Diana and Ariadne Webb had grown up in the East End together. They'd been at school together. They'd even made their forays into the world of pop music together, many decades ago. But that was before their friendship had gone sour. Words had been said, lines drawn in the sand, and now Diana, who prided herself on liking people, thoroughly disliked Ariadne Webb. It didn't even matter why any more.

Ariadne cut a stylish figure in her ACE Tours tour guide

outfit. It was classier and more luxurious than the faded blazers the Chartwell and Crouch team wore.

Her smooth brow creased in mock confusion. "This queue. This is for tourists. You know that, yes?"

Diana kept her expression composed. "A little mix up. Soon sorted."

Ariadne raised her chin. "You should perhaps have booked in advance?"

Diana pushed down her rage. "As I say. A mix up."

A younger man, also wearing an ACE Tours uniform, approached from the counter. He was blond and lithe, a cheetah in human form.

"Diana," Ariadne said. "Have I ever introduced you to Jed, my protégé?"

"We've not had the pleasure," said Jed. He had perfect white teeth and a roguish smile.

Ariadne gestured between them. "Diana, this is Jed Skirmish. Jed, this is the famous Diana Bakewell, an *old* friend."

"Ariadne speaks about you a lot," said Jed.

Diana nodded politely. "I leave the past where it belongs."

The queue was going nowhere, and Diana had no choice but to stay put. But Ariadne could sense Diana's discomfort and clearly wanted to wallow in it.

"We don't usually have to buy tickets," she said. "I know Glynn, the operations manager. He just gives us what we need. Do you know Glynn?"

"I don't know Glynn," Diana replied through gritted teeth.

"Really?"

"Really."

"Because you know everyone, don't you? That's your thing. Diana Bakewell, the woman who knows everyone. And here's me, little Ariadne Webb, and I happen to have connections you don't." She laughed. "Oh, listen to me rabbiting on! You and me, gossiping like the last twenty years never happened. I can see you're busy. Later, Diana."

She walked off, Jed in tow, then turned, a thoughtful expression on her face.

"Of course," she said. "I could get you the tickets you need. How many do you want? Twenty? Thirty?"

"Seven," replied Diana before she could stop herself.

"Seven." Another laugh. "That's barely any. I could get you seven tickets like..." She clicked her elegant fingers. "I could, couldn't I?"

More than anything, Diana wanted to tell Ariadne to shove off and take her flaming tickets with her. But the truth was that she did need tickets for the London Eye, and she needed them now.

"Will you do that?" she asked, her voice flat.

"Would you like me to?" Ariadne replied with similar coldness.

Diana swallowed. "That would be very helpful. And... what would you want in return?"

"Nothing, Diana. Seriously. Just a thank you."

Diana eyed her.

Ariadne stepped closer. "*Thank you, Ariadne.* Can you do that, Diana?"

Diana held her gaze. She forced a "Thank you, Ariadne," from her lips.

Ariadne's smile widened. "Anything for a friend." She turned towards the counter. "Glynn! Can you sort out Miss Bakewell here with – what was it? – seven tickets?"

Ariadne's fingers brushed Diana's upper arm.

"Truly a pleasure," she said and swept out.

A fresh-faced man at the counter beckoned Diana over and

presented her with seven genuine tickets. She thanked him numbly and headed out to her group, joining the throng circulating outside. Tickets in one hand, phone in the other, she bent to message Zaf to ask where he was, and didn't see the man in the hat until she walked right into him.

They collided and he stumbled, the green felt fedora falling from his head and the pair of postcards he was carrying tumbling to the ground.

"Oh, my goodness," said Diana. "I am sorry."

"Damn well watch where you're going," he muttered.

He went after his hat, so she bent to collect his postcards. They were old postcards, depicting fairies in an art nouveau style, quite beautiful in their own way. She passed them to the man as he furiously brushed off his hat. He had a deeply lined face, his nose large with age, and in spite of the hat and the paisley silk scarf around his neck, there was something shabby about him.

His sharp eyes glared at her as he snatched the postcards from her hand and hurried into the crowd.

"Sorry again," she called, but he had gone.

She looked about, remembered herself and messaged Zaf once more.

CHAPTER FIVE

Zaf had no idea if clean light was even possible in central London, but he swung through the crowds, leading the group to an ideal photography spot. He arranged them into various groups and posed them against the trees and the commercial buildings, turning them this way and that to capture them at their best.

The superiority with which the men looked at him eased once he was taking photos. Taking orders from a photographer was apparently preferable to chit-chatting with a lowly commoner.

"So you've all known each other a long time?" he asked.

"I've known this man all of my life." Alexsei put a hand on Kamran's shoulder, his expression solemn.

Kamran laughed. "Sadly, my son has inherited my sense of humour. But we three are old school friends." He gestured at Oxnard and Errol.

Oxnard puffed out his chest and gripped his lapels as Zaf took another photo. "The School of St Julian the Hospitaller, here in London."

"All of you?" Zaf glanced over his camera at Robin.

"I'm not one of these gentlemen," she said. "I had the pleasure of serving as valet to Mr Tristram Ramsgate, a fellow St Julian's alumnus."

"He's not here?"

"He is not," said Errol in his clipped South African accent. "But he's the reason we're all here today."

"Ah. I see..."

"Are we done doing photos or not, eh?" Errol snapped.

"Sorry," said Zaf. "A few more. School photo!" He got the men to huddle close. Robin stood to the side with a serene smile.

Just as he was running out of excuses to keep taking pictures, his phone buzzed with a message from Diana.

You can return now, I have valid tickets. Paul K sourced dudes.

Zaf smiled: *dudes* must had been auto-corrected from *duds*. Typical Paul Kensington.

He looked up at Kamran, hoping he was making a good impression. Alexsei hadn't referred to him as his boyfriend yet. Had he overstated his dad's acceptance of a gay son? Was he embarrassed by Zaf? Would Kamran be horrified that his son's boyfriend was just a poor black British *dude*?

Zaf shook his head: no time for doubt now. He had a job to do.

He gestured towards the river. "My colleague, Diana, will meet us back at the Eye."

As they walked, Robin slipped into step beside him.

"Just so you know, this is the anniversary of Mr Ramsgate's death," she muttered. "They – we – meet to commemorate and celebrate his life every year."

"I'm sorry," Zaf said. "I didn't mean to offend."

"You didn't know. It was an accidental death that shocked us all deeply. We grieve in our own ways."

"OK. Right. Sorry again. And..."

"Yes?" she said.

"A valet. That's like an Alfred the Butler type thing?"

She tilted her head. "Alfred the Butler was a butler. A valet is personally attached to the individual rather than the household. Like Jeeves in *Jeeves and Wooster*."

Zaf didn't know what *Jeeves and Wooster* was but he guessed he could ask Diana.

Robin moved on and Alexsei took her place beside Zaf.

"Killed by his own automated fire safety systems," he said.

"What?"

"Old Tristram Ramsgate. Owned a secure storage facility further down the Thames. An alarm was triggered while he was in one of the rooms and the system flooded it with halon gas. He was suffocated to death."

Zaf looked at Alexsei. *Nasty.*

Alexsei raised an eyebrow. "Just in case you were curious."

Diana was waiting at the entrance. She led them along the walkways and towards the capsules.

Zaf looked around the group. "Have you all been on this before?"

There were cautious nods all round, as though these wealthy men were embarrassed to admit they had engaged in something so ordinary.

"The supermodel Kate Moss has ridden on the London Eye at least twenty-five times," Diana told them as their capsule approached. "But I believe the celebrity record goes to Jessica Alba, who's been on more than thirty times."

"Who?" said Oxnard.

"The actress," said Errol. "We met her at that Chaumet party in Paris last summer."

"Oh, the American? Nice enough girl, I suppose."

They all stepped inside, hurrying to catch the constantly-moving pod. The doors closed and the noise of London's south bank was shut off, plunging them into silence.

The wheel continued onward. The men spread out across the lozenge-shaped cabin, moving to the windows that would soon give them views across the Thames and the great city. They ignored the other tourists inside the pod, accustomed to behaving as if they were the only people in the room.

"Anyone else think it's like being inside a massive hamster ball?" Zaf asked.

Oxnard Pike grunted. Errol van Blerk barked a laugh.

The valet, Robin, ran her hands over the curved window. "We are cocooned," she said. "Unopenable windows. Nothing in, nothing out."

"Wouldn't want anyone falling to their deaths," said Errol with a wink. He turned to Kamran Dadashov. "Well, Kamran. You tend to lead on these things."

Kamran clapped his hands together. "Very well. Let us begin."

CHAPTER SIX

As the capsule on the London Eye rose higher, revealing sights of Westminster Bridge, the Houses of Parliament and Cleopatra's Needle on the far bank, Kamran turned his back on the view and addressed them all.

"Once again, we three are gathered. We have the incomparable Robin Silversmith as our judge, as well as my son, Alexsei, and these two hired helpers to assist us. Our requirements in the coming days are somewhat specific, and now it is time to explain."

Diana smiled politely, listening as Mr Dadashov continued.

"The Tradition, as we call it, was set in motion on the day of Tristram's funeral. Each year we mark the passing of our friend by taking part in The Tradition."

He paused and looked out at the view. No one spoke.

"The Tradition is a set of challenges that hark back to that time. Each of us was building an empire—"

"Oh, we're emperors now?" said Errol.

Kamran gave him a look. "—and those days marked significant milestones for us all. If I remember correctly, Errol bought his first gym on the day of the funeral. Oxnard took the rest of us to one of his favourite memorabilia shops. And I? Well, I ate so many egg sandwiches at the wake that it haunted my dreams for weeks."

"We've only ever had your word on that one, old man," said Oxnard with a smile.

"The origins of The Tradition might *seem* trivial," said Kamran, "but we take it seriously. It is a game of strategy and skill, and open only to us three."

Errol nodded. "I scheduled my knee surgery around this."

"We put our hearts and souls into this challenge," Kamran continued. "As well as our considerable wealth. Each of us may select a helper for the challenge." He eyed Diana and Zaf. "Now you'll understand why we need to tell you all of this."

"So, wait," said Zaf. "We're your helpers in these challenges? That we know nothing about?"

Kamran nodded. "Three contestants, three helpers. The only pieces in the game. Alexsei, Diana and Zaf, is it? We will decide our teams shortly, and Ms Silversmith will oversee everything."

Robin turned to Diana and Zaf. "I ensure that rules are followed, I curate any recordings for the archive and I ultimately decide the winner, who will take possession of the valued prize."

"Tristram's ashes," said Kamran. "The winner displays them for a year."

Oxnard's gaze was on Robin. "Robin was Tristram's valet, and we all hold her in the highest possible regard."

Errol snorted. "What he really means to say is that we've all tried to hire Robin, but she won't be bought."

Robin gave a small smile. Diana wondered what motivated her, if it wasn't money.

"Robin," said Oxnard, "as adjudicator, maybe you can provide an overview of the three challenges?"

She inclined her head in a half-bow. "Of course, Mr Pike. There are three challenges over three days. The Postcard Challenge, the Egg Sandwich Challenge and the final one: The Race. The players lodge together over the three days, to enable discussion of strategy. I believe Mr van Blerk has made his luxury spa on Manchester Street available."

Errol nodded.

"Monitoring will be done via bodycams, which you'll all wear while working on a challenge."

Zaf raised a hand. Robin turned to him.

"If it's about toilet visits, you can pause the camera for five minutes at a time," she said.

Zaf shrugged and dropped his hand.

The valet surveyed the group. "This seems like a good time to pick our teams, don't you think?"

CHAPTER SEVEN

THE VALET STOPPED TALKING and the players surveyed each other. Errol rubbed his hands together. "Right. Tell us about our helpers, Robin."

Robin looked at Alexsei. "You have all met Alexsei Dadashov. He has an understated steadiness which will be valuable. Of course he will be loyal to his father, but I believe he has a personal honour which will ensure he applies his best efforts to assist whoever he is teamed with."

Robin turned to Zaf, who shuffled in place. Diana smiled, watching.

"Zaf has demonstrated good-natured professionalism," Robin said. "Does his youthful energy pose a risk in certain situations? Perhaps a small one."

Zaf's expression flickered. Robin's gaze moved on to Diana, who braced herself.

"Diana has maturity and experience," Robin said. "She is resourceful and thinks on her feet. And I imagine she knows how to exploit society's tendency to ignore women of a certain age."

"Society's what?" said Oxnard.

"She can be invisible in a crowd," replied Robin. She smiled at the helpers. "I'm sorry to describe you all in such candid terms, but it's part of my role. Gentlemen, I hope that helps you in your selection. Perhaps you can come to an agreement?"

Zaf looked thoughtful. "Youthful energy, eh? I might get that on a t-shirt."

The three men moved to the end of the capsule to confer. Diana looked past them and realised they were at the top of the wheel. Away to the east, following the course of the Thames, the pod took in views of St Paul's Cathedral, Tower Bridge and the soaring glass edifice of the Shard.

Diana went to the window and pulled a small pair of folding binoculars from her bag. She fiddled with them, picking out more detail.

"We have decided," said Oxnard.

Diana turned around.

"Oxnard will partner with my son," said Kamran. "Errol will partner with Diana. And *I* will partner with Zaf."

Diana eyed Errol van Blerk. She hoped she could be of value to him and that the experience wouldn't leave a bitter taste in both their mouths.

"Looking forward to it," said Zaf.

"Now, my champion," Kamran said, "as a tour guide, perhaps you could tell us what we're looking at." He held out a hand to draw Zaf to the viewing window.

"First," said Zaf, "please note that there are thirty-two capsules on the London Eye, one for each of the boroughs of London. Each capsule weighs ten tonnes. The capsules are numbered one to thirty-three, missing out unlucky number thirteen. I didn't check to see which one we were in as we entered..."

While Zaf spoke, Diana returned to the view. Below them was the jetty where Oxnard Pike's yacht was moored. It was smaller than some of the transport boats but larger than any other pleasure craft, perhaps longer even than the clippers that ferried foot passengers up and down the river.

She adjusted the focus to bring the yacht into clear view. The *Silver Salmon*. There was someone moving about on deck, wearing a heavy coat and green broad-brimmed hat. She'd seen that hat before: the man with the postcards she'd bumped into.

"There's someone on your boat, Mr Pike," she said.

The man was on the middle deck at the edge of a lounge area towards the aft of the boat. There was something furtive in the way he looked about before stepping inside and disappearing from sight.

Diana turned to her companions.

"Mr Pike," she repeated. "There's someone on your boat."

He waved a hand in dismissal. "A standing crew of twelve."

Diana shook her head. "Not crew." Crew wouldn't have been dressed like that. And besides, the postcard man...

She looked back at the boat. No one there. She frowned. Where was he?

She adjusted the binoculars again just as he reappeared through the entrance he'd gone in by, thrown back at speed as though he'd been punched. He slammed into the railing and pivoted. Diana tightened her grip on the binoculars as he tipped over the railing and fell off the side of the boat into the Thames. Diana saw spray and a spreading circle of foamy water.

She pulled the binoculars from her face, her heart racing. "Oh, my goodness."

Robin was at her side. "Are you alright, Diana?"

Diana pointed at the yacht. "Someone just fell off the yacht." She raised the binoculars again. The yacht was in silence, the water still.

"My yacht?" said Oxnard.

"Your yacht. He was pushed." Diana looked between the faces of the three wealthy men and their helpers. "Didn't you see? Did no one see?"

She trained the binoculars on the water, sweeping up and down, hoping to spot a head bobbing up, someone pulling themselves out.

There was nothing. Nothing at all.

"Are you sure you saw something, madam?" said Oxnard.

Diana frowned. *Of course I did.*

"I must phone the police." She pulled out her phone and dialled the emergency services. Her gaze remained on the water, waiting for movement.

CHAPTER EIGHT

Diana spoke as calmly as she could to the emergency services operator. She was shaken but she knew London and could describe the position of the jetty with pinpoint accuracy.

Their three wealthy employers hovered nearby, listening as she spoke. After a few moments, they were showing signs of restlessness.

"Shall I continue describing what we can see?" Zaf asked, his tone wary.

Oxnard was leaning against the glass. "I don't want the police crawling all over my yacht," he muttered.

"Yes," Kamran said. "Continue, young helper."

Zaf carried on describing the sights from the pod while Diana stayed on the line, describing what she had seen for the third time.

As the pod began its descent, a boat came speeding up the river, an S-shaped wake of water behind it. It approached the *Silver Salmon* and a police officer leaned over the prow to inspect the water.

She watched as several police officers arrived from across

Jubilee Gardens and searched the water from the shore. One officer hurried up the gangplank to the *Silver Salmon* and into the yacht.

How could a person fall into the river and be swallowed up so completely? It seemed unnerving that it could happen here, in her city. Diana had never thought of the Thames as something to be feared. Viewed, admired, even ignored, but never feared.

"Hello?" said the operator.

"I'm still here," Diana said.

"There will be officers at the exit to the London Eye. Could you identify yourself to them as you leave?"

"Yes, of course."

The operator ended the call.

Zaf was still in full flow. He was pointing out the bronze lion head mooring rings along the wall of Victoria Embankment. "... and the old saying goes that 'when the lions drink, London sinks'."

"Meaning?" said Oxnard.

"If the Thames has risen that high," said Kamran, "then we're all in trouble."

Zaf's lecture on London continued as they stepped out of the pod. Two police officers were indeed waiting for her: a woman in regular police gear and a bearded man in dark blue combat fatigues and a slender lifejacket.

Diana gave Zaf an apologetic look and went over to the officers.

"I'm Diana Bakewell. I phoned in a report of the person in the water."

"Right," said the bearded officer. "Well, first up, thank you. We'd rather people called 999 even when there's nothing wrong than suspect they've seen something but dismiss it."

She frowned. "He definitely fell in. I saw him. I recognised him."

"You know him?"

"I saw him here before we got on the Eye. He had a green hat. A felt hat, like a fedora."

The officers exchanged glances. "Maybe you'd like to talk us through what happened," the female officer said.

They walked with Diana towards the jetty. She told them what she'd seen.

"... he flew backwards, like he'd been punched," she finished.

"You saw him fly backwards?" asked the woman.

"Yes."

"Fly backwards how?"

"Like someone had shoved him," she said. "Powerfully. As if someone had thrown him with all their might."

The policeman raised his hands to indicate the visible open back of the *Silver Salmon*. Now at ground level, Diana could see inside. Glass screen doors were drawn aside, offering a view right into the lounge area.

"Did you see the person who shoved him?"

"I saw no one."

"But you saw the man?"

"Yes. You've not found him?"

The policeman looked out over the river. "You'd be surprised at the speed of the current here. Can easily get up to eight knots."

"I'm afraid I don't know what that means."

"About ten miles an hour. Faster than any of us can swim. Faster than you can row." He consulted his watch. "If a body went in here and if it hasn't snagged on any structures, then it could be out beyond Canary Wharf and the Isle of Dogs already."

Diana noted the *if*. "You don't believe me, do you?"

The man smiled. "It's not a matter of believing you or not."

"We've spoken to the crew on the yacht," the woman said. "They saw no one at all." She gave Diana a curious look. "No one got on that boat."

"I saw him." Diana kept her voice low but determined.

"We see all kinds of things, don't we?" said the man. "The eye, the mind, they all play tricks on us." He wagged a finger at the London Eye above them. "And things can look different when you're way up there."

Diana felt hollow. They didn't believe her. They'd been nothing but polite, friendly and interested, but somehow that made it even worse.

She had seen a man fall from a boat to his almost certain death, and no one else believed it had even happened.

CHAPTER NINE

ZAF TRAILED behind the group of wealthy friends as they crossed Jubilee Gardens, making for a waiting limousine on Belvedere Road.

Robin Silversmith, the former valet, was at the front. "The challenges do not officially commence until tomorrow," she told the men. "You have today to put any affairs in order."

"You make it sound like we're all going to kick the bucket," said Oxnard.

She smiled. "This is your last chance to take care of your own business before we're locked in together." She raised an eyebrow. "But I have taken the liberty of booking a table at Alain Ducasse's restaurant at the Dorchester, if any of you wish to partake."

"I could go for a spot of lunch," said Errol.

"Some pleasant chit-chat before the serious business," added Kamran. He turned to take in his son and Zaf. "You are all welcome." He frowned, realising the same thing as Zaf. Where had Diana gone?

"Eish!" said Errol. "My helper's already legged it."

Oxnard and Kamran laughed.

Zaf backed away. "I'd best go check where she is. Enjoy your lunch, everyone."

He gave Alexsei a final look then hurried back towards the Eye. Oxnard shouted something about his 'yacht' but Zaf didn't quite catch it.

The police were no longer on board the yacht. There was still a police launch turning slow circles in the river while officers looked out over the water. There was no sign of Diana.

Zaf scanned the thickening crowds and pushed back along the Queen's Walk between the park and the river. A bare-chested acrobat with Jamaican flag leggings was loudly warming up the crowd around him in preparation for his act. From somewhere, a busker crooned the song *Hallelujah*. Smells rose from the temporary fast-food outlets down by the Hungerford Bridge. He'd never find Diana in amongst all this.

He pulled out his phone, and was about to call her when the crowd parted and there she was. Diana sat by the balustrade overlooking the river while a caricaturist seated opposite her worked on a sketch pad.

"Here you are!" Zaf declared, a little miffed that he'd been worrying while she was getting her picture drawn.

Diana looked at him, her face tight. "Do you know, I can't find a single person who saw the man on the boat. Not one! I've asked up and down this whole area."

"I'm... I'm sorry. I didn't see him either."

"At least you don't think I made it up. The police did."

Zaf frowned. Did he believe her? No one else had seen anything, and they'd been right above the scene. If a man had fallen in, surely *someone* would have seen it?

But, no, this was Diana Bakewell.

"I don't think you made it up," he said. "If no one in the world saw it but you, I'd still believe you."

She gave him a nod of thanks. The caricaturist turned her board to show Diana.

"Oh, yes," Diana said. "He was perhaps a little bit more lined around the eyes. They were smaller eyes, I suppose. Staring, as if he needed glasses. A disapproving stare."

The drawing wasn't of Diana at all. The artist had produced an image of an older man under a broad hat, wearing a worn and miserable expression.

"Elena here is helping me draw a picture of our victim."

"Wow," said Zaf. "You must have had really powerful binoculars."

She shook her head. "I saw him before we got on the Eye. Well, I saw a man wearing that hat. Can't imagine there's many like it round here."

The artist finished the sketch and Diana paid her in cash. She took the portrait.

"Hold still," said Zaf and took a photo of the image.

"Good." Diana rolled the thick paper up into a tube.

"What now? We go around asking people if they've seen him?"

Diana pursed her lips. "We've lost our tour party for the day."

"They've gone to the Dorchester for lunch," Zaf told her. "We were invited, too."

"Shame. The chicken quenelles are lovely."

Zaf gave an exasperated laugh. "I might have known you'd eaten there already."

She eyed him with a twinkle. "I *might* have a friend in the kitchen."

He laughed and they turned to walk together.

"I'd like to get a look at that boat," said Diana.

"Oxnard's yacht? What d'you think you'll learn?"

"This chap went aboard, regardless of what the police insinuated. And if he went aboard it was either because he was gripped by random curiosity or for a specific reason."

Zaf resisted the urge to take hold of her arm. He didn't want her thinking he was pulling her back. "You know... you don't have to do this."

Diana stopped walking, a family group almost crashing into them from behind. Zaf muttered an apology.

"I beg your pardon?" Diana said to him, oblivious to the two children trying to squeeze past them.

He waved in the direction of the mooring jetty. "You saw a man fall in the water and, yeah, it does look like he drowned. It's sad. But you've done everything you need to do. You don't need to find him or find out why he was there. You've done your bit."

There was an intensity in Diana's eyes Zaf didn't often see. "They *didn't* believe me!" she said in a low hiss.

"I know. I understand."

"You don't understand. I am what they call *a woman of a certain age*. Not old yet, but I can see it coming." She huffed out a sigh. "My mum warned me this would happen. That valet, Robin, she had it right. The one superpower I have left in my arsenal is that the world never pays attention to the grey-haired woman."

"It's more of an ash-blonde if anything and—"

"They ignored me. Politely! Oh, that was almost the worst of it." She looked away. "I met Ariadne Webb earlier."

"Ah."

Zaf knew of Diana's antipathy towards Ariadne, even if he didn't know the full reasons for it. There were aspects of her life – Ariadne Webb, her old friend Pascal Palmer and her old boss Morris Walker who'd somehow ended up in prison – she kept secret.

"I was made to look a fool this morning," she said. "We had no tickets and, for once, there were no favours I could call in to fix it. I had to rely on the kindness of Ariadne bloody Webb to get us tickets." She shook her head. "To be powerless, ignored, invisible. You can't imagine."

Zaf had to suppress a smile. "Oh, yeah, yeah. Your black gay friend has no idea what it feels like to be marginalised."

She looked at him. He raised an eyebrow. She laughed, which was as good a reaction as any. She gripped his arm tight, affectionately.

"I need to do this thing," she said. "I want to find out what happened to that man on Oxnard Pike's yacht."

Zaf got it. "Fair enough. Lead on."

They continued along the south bank to the jetty and reached it just in time to see the *Silver Salmon* pull away and move out into the Thames.

Diana tutted. "Fiddlesticks."

There was a man working on the jetty. "Oi, mate!" Zaf called over. "Where's that boat off to?"

The man gave him a *what business is it of yours?* look.

"He left his auntie behind!" said Zaf, pointing at Diana.

The man pointed. "Savoy Pier. By—"

"Just across the river," Diana said. She narrowed her eyes, clearly looking for the quickest walking route.

"We really doing this?" Zaf said.

She gave him a smile. "Time to test out my invisibility superpower."

CHAPTER TEN

"They could have decided to move the yacht for a load of reasons," said Zaf as they crossed the Thames via the pedestrian bridge beyond Jubilee Gardens. Diana had used the Golden Jubilee Bridge many times; it would lead them to Embankment and the Savoy Pier.

"True," Diana replied. "I expect it's prohibited to moor by the Eye for long."

"Or they're moving to be nearer to where Oxnard Pike is."

She shook her head, grimacing as a train rumbled over the Charing Cross Bridge next to them. The Dorchester was northeast of here, opposite Hyde Park. "Or they just want to get away from the police and the scene created by that *mad old lady*."

Zaf shook his head. "You're really taking this to heart."

Diana pursed her lips. "I don't like being ignored and dismissed. Which reminds me, I must call my mum later. It's been a few days."

They hurried down the steps at the far side of the bridge

and crossed the road to reach the riverbank. Zaf stopped, eyeing a small boat pulling up at the pier ahead of them.

"You're just going to wander in?" he said.

"Let's see what happens. You coming?"

He shook his head. "Like you say, women of a certain age can make themselves invisible. Young black men, not so much. Back home I've been stopped by the police enough times just for standing around."

She gave his arm a sympathetic pat then strolled down the steps by the embankment wall and onto the pier. No one gave her so much as a glance.

There were boats moored up along the length of the floating pier. The smallest were just pleasure craft, but the ones that could be called yachts came in a variety of sizes, with the *Silver Salmon* possibly the largest. Three visible decks made the vessel as large as a house.

Some of Diana's extended family worked the river and pretty much lived on boats, but Diana wasn't familiar with them. She knew the river but had no real knowledge of the boats that used it.

There was a gangplank lowered from the yacht to the pier and, again, no sign of any crew. Swinging her brolly, Diana walked to the gangplank and climbed aboard at the stern, wondering if there was a word for the deck she was on.

A short flight of stairs led up to what seemed to be the main deck, with its sitting area from which she'd seen the fedora-wearing man violently ejected.

Her phone buzzed: Zaf.

"Everything OK?" she asked, pressing her phone to her ear.

"How's it going?" he whispered.

"Fine. I'm in the lounge bit where the man was. And why are you whispering?"

A pause. "So what's it like?" he asked in a more normal voice.

She surveyed the interior saloon area. It had expensive wood flooring, white leather seating and a kind of Scandinavian minimalist chic. The main items of interest were the artworks. There were impressionist paintings, of bright landscapes and carefree people, and a number of sculptures. There was a roughly-executed bronze of a seated woman and, in the middle of the room, a much smoother statue in iron or steel of a dog, seated as though waiting for the arrival of its owner.

Diana approached the closest paintings.

"Some nice art here. *After the Bath, Bazille*," she read.

"Frédéric Bazille?" said Zaf.

She shrugged. "Never heard of him."

"Genuine nineteenth-century impressionist. A lot of *en plein air* painting. That's painting outdoors to you and me." A pause. "Tell me it's real."

She looked at the image of the woman and her maid. "It *looks* real. You do know a lot about art."

"I didn't study Art History for nothing."

Diana looked around, thinking of what she'd seen from the pod. She stood in the centre of the room. There were banquette seats and low tables dotted around.

"So, the man came in here," she said. "If he stood here, then his assailant had to be about there." She gestured towards a space between the table, the wall and the dog statue. "He or she had to have come from that way."

She moved forward through the yacht, checking for signs of security cameras. None were visible. A narrow corridor led to a staircase where she could go below decks, up to the top deck or forward to one of the private cabins. While she was deciding where to go next, she heard voices above.

"Just say you were watching football, Phillipe," said a man.

"You want me to say I was watching football?" enquired a second man with a French accent.

"I want you to admit you were watching football."

"You know I had duties elsewhere."

"Either you were shirking your duties in front of the TV, Phillipe, or whoever phoned the police was just making things up."

"Captain," said the Frenchman, his tone offended, "you think it is more likely that I was 'shirking' my duties while some stranger no one else saw came on board? You think that is more likely? Than some old lady making things up? After our little chat last week? *Please.*"

"Marseilles are playing Paris Saint-Germain today," replied the captain.

"I had no idea." Diana could hear the lie in the Frenchman's voice.

Zaf was still on the line. "What's going on?" he asked.

Diana was about to whisper a reply when she heard a footstep on the stairs. A foot clad in a deck shoe and a long white sock appeared.

She held her breath and hurried back along the corridor and into the lounge.

"Diana? What's going on?"

She shook her head and plunged her phone into the pocket of her uniform blazer. She couldn't risk them hearing him.

She reached the open rear exit and was about to step off the boat again when she heard the captain's voice.

"Excuse me."

Grimacing, Diana turned. The man was youngish but balding, every bit the sailor in a crisp white shirt and navy-blue shorts.

"Ah, there you are," she said. "I was just admiring the –"
She waved her hand at one of the paintings. "– the Bazille. I
prefer his *en plain air* stuff myself."

"Who are you and what are you doing here?"

Diana drew herself up. "You left the London Eye. I was
talking with the officers and realised I still had some questions
that needed answering."

"You are with the police?" he said.

She didn't want to lie. "Phillipe should have been carrying
his duties out in this area, shouldn't he?"

The captain frowned. "The steward's duty includes this
area."

Ah. Both of them, not lying, but not telling the full truth
either.

"But if he'd been here he would have seen the intruder,"
she said. "Or was it a guest?"

"There were no guests in this area," the man replied.
"Now, I will need to see some ID."

She looked about, committing the space to memory. "I
assume you've got all of this insured," she said, waving her
brolly at the art. "Some lovely pieces." She patted the dog statue's head. It did have a very endearing expression.

"ID." The captain's mouth was set in a line.

"I don't seem to have police ID on me," she said. "I'd best
go find it." She turned to step off the boat and walked as casu-
ally as she could down the gangplank and away along the pier.

There was a shouted "Hey!" behind her but no one
followed. She didn't look back.

Zaf was waiting on the stone steps leading up to Waterloo
Bridge. Diana hooked her arm through his and took a deep
breath.

"That was close," she muttered.

"I heard all of it," he said. "You've got some nerve, Diana Bakewell. Learn anything?"

She considered as they started to walk across the bridge. "The steward wasn't where he should have been. Someone lied to the police, possibly just to avoid trouble with the boss. Also, Oxnard has some very nice art."

"You think our mystery man was an art thief?"

Diana thought about the sour-faced man in the hat. The fedora hat and silk scarf could have belonged to a man who appreciated the finer things in life.

She shrugged. There was no evidence either way.

"I don't know," she admitted.

CHAPTER ELEVEN

By the time he and Diana arrived back at the depot, Zaf felt wrung out. The day had been intense, and when he'd texted Alexsei to see if they were needed at the Dorchester, the reply had worried him. *We're fine here. See you in the morning.*

It was one thing not needing their professional services, but why wouldn't Alexsei want him to join them and get to know his father better?

Stop worrying, he told himself. Alexsei was busy. And he'd trusted Zaf with arranging the tour surrounding the Tradition. Whatever that would turn out to be.

Paul Kensington was taking photos of the depot's interior when they entered. He lowered his camera.

"How are our new well-heeled clients?" he asked, an unhealthy glint in his eye. "Tell me you've persuaded them to buy more of our packages."

"We have not," said Diana.

"Remember that cross-sell and up-sell are the new watchwords."

Her stare was hard. "We came close to losing them when we tried to get onto the London Eye with pirated tickets."

"With what?"

"Where on earth did you get them from, Paul? I had to pull out all the stops to get replacements and repair the situation."

Paul opened his mouth, his face pale, then shook his head as one of his ideas hit him. "Did you pay full price for those replacements? We should seek out discounts—"

"I sorted it. You miss the point, Paul. We should not put important client relationships at risk by engaging with scalpers and crooks."

"Right. I will have to look into what happened there. Thank you for bringing it to my attention."

Zaf headed for the kitchen break room.

"Don't forget about cross-selling and up-selling, will you?" Paul called after them. "We need to get our utilisation rates up."

Zaf rolled his eyes and Diana sighed.

The driver Newton Crombie was in the break room. He'd made a pot of tea and was sifting through a packet of digestive biscuits, sorting them into two boxes according to how damaged they were.

"Shall I pour?" said Zaf. He poured three cups from the fat glazed teapot.

"I need to go and phone my mum," said Diana, taking a cuppa in one hand and waggling her phone in the other. "I've not spoken to her in a while. I'll just check she's alright."

Zaf had briefly met Diana's mum, Beverley, or Bev, as she'd told Zaf to call her. The woman might be in her late eighties but he doubted Diana needed to fear for her welfare. Bev struck Zaf as a woman who'd got tougher and more resilient with age, even if she refused to set foot outside her own little corner of London.

"What a day." He dropped into one of the little seats. Gus appeared from nowhere and hopped onto his lap, ready to provide some comfort. Zaf tickled him under the chin and Gus headbutted him in return.

"Did everything go OK?" asked Newton. "It's given me the opportunity to get my beauties in tip-top condition. Paul even took some photos of them."

Newton's 'beauties' were his buses. The depth of affection he held for them was astonishing, disconcerting even. Newton had a family at home and Zaf sometimes wondered if he loved them as much as his buses.

"Glad you've had a good day," Zaf said. "I'm sure Gus here has been super helpful."

Gus's brand of super-helpfulness mostly involved standing in the way and demanding attention.

Newton grunted. "I think Gus has been busy in his own way. Can I show you something?"

"I guess so."

Newton went to the cupboard under the sink and pulled out a carrier bag. It was full of women's shoes.

Zaf raised an eyebrow. "Didn't know you were into women's shoes, Newton."

Newton tutted. "Gus keeps bringing them in."

"What d'you mean?"

Newton frowned. "I'm not sure which word you're struggling with. I'm saying that, while some cats bring in dead rats and pigeons, our Gus seems to have been bringing shoes into the depot and... well, presenting them to me as gifts."

Zaf pulled out a couple of the shoes. "I'm no expert on women's fashion, but these look expensive."

"These are 'Christian Louboutin'," said Newton. "This one's a 'Prada' and this is a 'Jimmy Choo'." He listed the designer brands like someone who'd only just learned their names.

Zaf tickled Gus under the chin. "Where've they come from, Gus?"

Newton shrugged. "You know what he's like. One minute he's there and the next he's gone off somewhere. It can't be too far away, it's not like he disappears for hours on end."

"Why shoes?" Zaf asked Gus.

"I sometimes think Gus enjoys our reactions," said Newton. "But more to the point, what do I do with them all?"

"Maybe he's been raiding a shoe shop?"

"I don't think there's any near here."

Zaf shrugged. "Maybe a rich woman's been leaving her window open and Gus has been raiding her wardrobe?"

"But they're all different sizes," said Newton. "I have this horrible image of Gus mugging women in the street, wrestling their shoes from them and... and..."

"It's not a likely scenario, is it?" said Zaf.

"Well, I'd welcome a better suggestion. This is quite the mystery."

Zaf nodded. There'd been enough mysteries for one day already.

CHAPTER TWELVE

Zaf walked home to Eccleston Square in Pimlico. It was quicker to get the tube or bus but there was no better way to get a feel for his adopted city than to walk its streets. Those streets were quiet today, the cold having sent most of London underground.

The house he shared with Diana was a grand building dating back to the early Victorian period. The high white houses of Eccleston Square, with barely a gap between them, crowded round the lush greenery of the park at its centre.

Zaf waved to Nichola, who was tending the gardens as usual, and jogged up the steps to their house. He entered to hear music coming from the open door of Alexsei's downstairs flat.

"Zaf?" called Alexsei.

Zaf smiled. "It's me." He entered to find Alexsei in the living room, lounging in his favourite curved swan chair. He folded the newspaper he was reading and reached forward to pour Zaf a glass of iced tea from a jug on the coffee table.

"Thought you could do with a drink."

Zaf took it. "Iced tea, in February? Is there alcohol in this?"

"It can be arranged."

"I thought you'd still be at the Dorchester."

"A light lunch. Robin and I left them to it after the coffees." Alexsei was looking at him expectantly. "So, I hope meeting my father and his friends wasn't too much of an ordeal."

"I think I'm still trying to process what went on today. The whole setup of your dad's friends and their peculiar game, the way Robin described us all like we weren't there. And then the person Diana saw falling off Oxnard's yacht."

Zaf took a long gulp of his tea, slumping onto the leather sofa.

Alexsei grunted and gave a tight nod.

Zaf leaned forward. "You do believe her, don't you?"

"She is Diana. Of course I believe her. It is strange to imagine that such a thing could happen out in the open in central London and nobody else sees it. Strange... but not impossible."

"Your dad barely noticed me," said Zaf. "Does he know that we're—"

"An item?" Alexsei pursed his lips. "No. I have not told him."

"Oh." Zaf fell back, wondering if he should be angry.

"My father is complicated."

"Complicated how?"

"He, like me, had the benefit of British education."

"The school of St Julian?"

A nod. "Julian the Hospitaller, here in London. My grandfather, who made his money working for the state oil company, invested heavily in his only son. Legacy is important to him. My father's portfolio is diverse. Engineering, electronics, research."

"Property," said Zaf, gesturing to the house about them.

"He has his fingers in many pies. And as I say, legacy is important to him." Alexsei wasn't making eye contact.

Zaf studied Alexsei's face. "Does your father want grandchildren?"

Alexsei tilted his head, still not meeting Zaf's eye.

Zaf frowned. "He knows you're gay but he still somehow expects you to find a nice wife and have lots of little Dadashovs?"

Alexsei smiled sadly. "That sentiment has never been put into words before now."

Zaf gestured broadly at himself. "You may not have noticed but I'm not..."

Alexsei reached forward and squeezed Zaf's hand. "Life is never easy, is it?"

Zaf looked at his boyfriend, who was at least returning his gaze now. It wasn't even as if being gay meant Alexsei couldn't provide Kamran with grandchildren. Not that he and Zaf were anywhere near that point...

He shook his head. "So, I'm to be your shameful little secret."

"I am not ashamed," said Alexsei. "And there will be no nice wife. To thine own self be true, no?"

"But this week we're keeping it on the down low, huh?"

"Until my father's games are done. Then we will tell him."

Zaf downed the rest of his drink. His mind was racing.

"Oxnard," he said. "What kind of name is that?"

Alexsei grinned. "An old family one. In my experience, the rich hold onto everything, even weird names. You will see that Oxnard Pike is a man who likes nice things. He has one of the largest private collections of art in the world. Some truly obscure but valuable pieces, and he almost never lets anyone see them. Vermeers and Rembrandts that haven't been on display in decades. Estimates of his financial worth vary but they are all astronomically high."

"And I gather Errol is also into property," said Zaf.

"Very specific property. He inherited a uranium mine in the north-east of South Africa but his heart isn't in it. He's most interested in leisure. Hotels, resorts. That spa we're meeting at tomorrow. It's not far from your work."

"I'll be brutally honest," said Zaf, "I'm nervous about tomorrow. Not only did it feel like I was being picked for a team in PE but... I don't really know these kinds of people."

"These kinds?"

"Rich people."

Alexsei laughed. "Am I not a rich person?"

"Rich *old* people."

"My father is fifty-six."

"Like I said..."

Alexsei laughed again. "My father will want to win. He views this whole thing, the Tradition, life itself, as a great big chess game. He will plan and plan to win. Tomorrow you work with him and in his scheme you will be his most powerful piece. You can be his queen, can't you?"

"Me, a queen? Really?"

Alexsei gave him a wink. "Approach this as you approach everything else." He waved his hands.

Zaf laughed. "Approach it with jazz hands?"

"A little razzmatazz. You have used this expression to me, I think? It is where you leap in feet-first, lots of enthusiasm."

"I can do that." Zaf sighed. "I'm just scared they'll realise we're together and it'll turn out to be against the rules, some-how. And I'm a bit scared of Robin."

Alexsei shrugged as he poured them both another glass of

tea. "We don't owe Robin any explanation of ourselves. We will play the game and then we will tell my father about us. Makes sense, no?"

"I guess." Zaf was worried he'd disappoint both Alexsei and his dad, and that Kamran would be horrified by them being a couple.

But he kept that thought to himself.

CHAPTER THIRTEEN

In the morning, Zaf, Diana and Alexsei took the five-minute walk to the Serenity Haven Spa, where they'd agreed to meet the tour party.

The frontage was discreet and Zaf hesitated on the pavement, wondering if they'd got the right place.

"Exclusive," muttered Diana as she walked up the front steps.

Zaf shrugged. He'd never get into a place like this, not as a paying customer. And the Chartwell and Crouch uniform made it clear he wasn't one of those.

"It's OK," Alexsei muttered, taking his hand. "Nothing to be afraid of."

Zaf gave him a smile. Was he looking afraid?

The reception area was painted white with a sleek white counter running along the far end. Splashes of green came from foliage dotted artfully around the place.

"Hello, lovely souls." The receptionist's doll-like face was as immaculate as the decor. "Welcome to Serenity Haven. I'm Mindy."

"We are here to see Errol van Blerk," said Diana.

"Ah, you are some of his special guests. Diana, Zaf and Alexsei, isn't it?"

"Yes," said Zaf. He dropped Alexsei's hand and hid his surprise. *Be professional.*

"Let me show you the way. I'll give a little tour as we go." Mindy swept out from behind her desk. "Picture this: a restored Victorian townhouse filled with the warmth of a summer garden. That's our haven right here in Marylebone."

She waved a hand to indicate a corridor. "Our gym, a spiritual home for wellness warriors, is packed with the latest equipment to make your heart race and your spirits soar. High-energy workouts. Serene yoga sessions. But it's our spa sanctuary where the magic really happens." She turned to them with a smile. "Plush furnishings, calming soundscapes, the very best therapies: it's like a hug for your soul. This way."

The three of them followed the woman up a spiral staircase. Zaf eyed Alexsei, wondering if he'd been here before.

"Up on our rooftop retreat," said the receptionist, "you'll find a slice of paradise overlooking the city. It's your escape from the hustle and bustle. At Serenity Haven, we're all about creating moments."

"Is that so?" said Alexsei, a smile flickering on his lips.

"And every moment here," continued Mindy, "is a memory waiting to happen."

Alexsei raised an eyebrow at Zaf, who suppressed a snigger. "Right."

But cynic or not, Zaf couldn't deny that the rooftop terrace was beautiful. Pale sofas were arranged with precision masked as carelessness. Sections were screened off in a labyrinth of trellises and climbing plants, creating a sense of multiple private spaces. Zaf peered across and spotted the angled glass roof of the bus depot not more than two hundred metres away.

Mindy ushered them into a lounge area where Errol, Oxnard and Kamran sipped tea on sofas arranged in a generous U-shape.

"Howzit going?" called Errol, waving them over. "I hope Mindy explained that you have rooms here at your disposal for the coming days."

"She said a lot of things," replied Diana.

A nod. "I want you all to feel as welcome as possible here, so do ask if there's anything at all that you need."

"Thank you," said Zaf.

"We're keen to get started," said Alexsei.

"Sit down then," Errol told him. "Grab a pastry. The Moroccan *beghrir* are delicious. Robin's gonna talk us through our first task."

Once they were settled, Robin took the floor. Today, she had ditched yesterday's U-boat commander look for a formal waistcoat and narrow tie, which reminded Zaf of Marlene Dietrich.

"So today is the first day," she said, "and the first challenge. Let me explain why it's called the Postcard Challenge."

Robin reached behind her and pulled out an old, sepia postcard. She held it high. "Here we have a vintage postcard, chosen for last year's challenge. You can see that it has a view from the Lake District on the front, but what we're interested in is the address on the back."

She turned it to show them the faded, spidery writing. "It is an address on Kerrison Road in Ealing. The challenge that day was to buy a property near to that address."

"Sorry?" said Zaf. "Buy a property?"

Errol cracked a grin. "The winner of the challenge was the

one who could purchase a property close by. If more than one competitor secured a purchase, then the one who was closest would win."

"Oh my," muttered Diana.

"Oh my, indeed," said Robin. "Now, the postcard we select could bear an address anywhere in London. The postcards are vetted to ensure we can pinpoint the address on a modern map, but as long as that proviso is met, they could be anywhere within the city. "

"How do you select a postcard?" asked Diana.

"We have a dealer who prepares a selection for us. You might remember that Oxnard has a favourite memorabilia shop? It's over by the Charing Cross Road. We'll go there shortly to view them. We will pick a card at random, and that will form the basis for our challenge." Robin surveyed the group. "Any more questions?"

"Yes," said Diana. "Buying property usually takes quite a while. What do you mean when you say that we must secure the sale?"

Robin nodded. "Each team may engage with solicitors, estate agents and other legal professionals in order to prepare documents and progress the sale. What we need to declare a winner is a binding agreement to make the sale of the property. The other teams are at liberty to scrutinise any documents for loopholes, because this is a commitment that must be followed through." She looked up from the postcard. "It should be noted that this professional help may not be used for other, more general tasks. Part of the fun of the challenge is that only two people can work directly on finding a building's owner and then persuading them to sell."

Diana nodded. Zaf said nothing. The idea of buying a

property as part of a game... He looked at Alexsei, seeing his boyfriend in a new light.

"Good," said Robin. "If the rules are understood then please put on your bodycams and we can depart for the shop."

Zaf was reeling. London property was famously expensive, and here they were going off to buy some just for the glory of winning a game. It would be his job to help Kamran buy some London property. The father of his boyfriend, and clearly unfeasibly wealthy.

The bodycam was little more than a lapel button, a glassy-eyed flower.

"Bespoke cameras," said Robin, "designed by a very clever man I know in Reading. You'll barely know you're wearing them."

As Zaf pinned his on, Kamran approached him.

"Fighting fit, yes?" said Dadashov senior.

"Very much so, sir."

"It is Kamran, please."

Zaf smiled. "Kamran."

"I have everything planned. Just do precisely as I instruct and the day will be ours."

Zaf nodded. It wasn't as if he'd have the faintest idea where to start.

Errol slapped Zaf on the back on his way to the stairs. "Such confidence."

Zaf swallowed. How could Kamran be so confident? The task ahead of them was madness itself.

CHAPTER FOURTEEN

Two limos were waiting for them outside Serenity Haven. Diana looked at them, wondering how Newton felt about his beloved bus not getting a spin today.

Kamran and Oxnard climbed into the first, with their helpers Zaf and Alexsei. Diana followed Errol van Blerk and Robin Silversmith into the second.

"These things are wired for sound?" she asked.

"I can monitor all aspects of the task," Robin replied. "Obviously you will be careful to avoid saying anything that might disadvantage your partner."

Errol frowned. "There's nothing you can say to hurt or offend me. Water off a duck's back."

"As you say," replied Robin.

"Your spa is beautiful," Diana told him.

"It's alright," said Errol. "London's one of them places where you can tart anything up and slap a big price tag on it in the name of exclusivity. You should see the resort I'm building out in the UAE. Forget five stars. Six, seven."

Robin's cheek twitched. Diana glanced at her. What was the valet's opinion of these men's wealth?

She turned back to Errol. "I'll be sure to check it out."

Errol smiled. He smiled easily, Diana had noticed. "Win this week for me and I'll fly you out there for a month."

The limo pulled away and Diana relaxed into her seat. The seats were upholstered in soft leather, many times more comfortable than the seats of their vintage bus, but nowhere near as iconic.

"Your former employer, Mr Ramsgate," she said to Robin. "Do you mind telling me a little about him?"

Robin seemed briefly to fight surprise, before adopting her usual smooth expression.

"Tristram Ramsgate was a fine employer—"

"He was a school swot and a workaholic," interrupted Errol. "And one of my best mates as well, obviously."

"He inherited his father's company," continued Robin. "Food distribution and logistics. But he diversified. Never stopped."

That was what he *did*, thought Diana. But not who he *was*.

"He was a man whose brain fizzed with ideas and energy," Robin said. "He wanted to do everything. But inside, he was a shy and self-critical soul."

Errol shook his head. "He loved parties."

"He loved people," countered Robin, "and he wanted them to be happy. He married, twice, but neither worked out. He wanted to be all things to all people and perhaps struggled to be anything significant to one person. He tried every hobby and every game. He rode horses. He kept dogs. He learned the piano. He painted."

"He was bloody awful at all of them," said Errol.

Robin surprised Diana by laughing out loud, the first crack in her professional demeanour.

"Yes," she said. "He *was* awful at all of them. But he wanted to try everything. He seemed to know, more than any of us, that our time here is limited."

Errol sighed. "Hell, I miss him. We all do. When he died, we all wished..." He looked out of the window. "We'll drink to departed friends, later."

The limo slowed to a halt and Diana looked out. "Ah, Cecil Court." The cobblestoned Victorian passage off Charing Cross Road was familiar to her.

The driver opened the door for them and she followed Errol out and into the street with its faded charm. Behind weathered facades were antiquarian bookshops and vintage stores. Many a tour guide (*not* Diana) would wrongly point the street out as the inspiration for Diagon Alley from the Harry Potter stories. She could see why it was an appealing notion.

The other limo pulled up behind them and Robin led the six of them to a shop called *Stanley Grosvenor Memorabilia*. Signs above the windows declared that rare and collectable coins, stamps and postcards were for sale.

Diana smiled as they entered the shop, enjoying its old-fashioned glow. She imagined it as unchanged for a century or more. The woodwork was painted dark green with gold lettering. Medals and coins were arrayed on racks, sealed into protective plastic pouches, some on little velvet stands. Displays of envelopes and postcards with special stamps lined the walls.

Diana gave Zaf a nudge. He'd been staring, open-mouthed. He gave her a grin and clamped his mouth shut.

The interior was crowded with display cases, albums to leaf through, and boxes of postcards organised by location. Zaf drifted towards a Birmingham box, but the others were gath-ered at the glass counter.

"Welcome all of you," said the man behind the counter. He wore a shabby, threadbare suit and his white hair contrasted with his brown skin, lending him a distinguished air. "I shall close the shop for a moment so we're not disturbed while we select your postcard."

He bustled to the door and closed the latch, switching the sign to *Closed*. He turned to them, satisfied. Zaf moved away from the Birmingham box and joined the rest of them. Diana threw him a quick smile.

"Can I get you some tea first?" the shopkeeper asked. "Old Philbin is not entirely incompetent in the kitchen. Or would you rather I did that after you've selected your postcard?"

The friends glanced between themselves. Diana could sense their impatience.

"Postcards, fellow," said Oxnard. "We need to start."

"Very good." The shopkeeper opened the flap in the counter and invited them all through to the back room.

CHAPTER FIFTEEN

IN THE BACK room of the memorabilia shop, storage boxes were piled so densely on the shelves that they almost blocked out the light. In the centre of the room was a large wooden desk with a leather top, empty apart from a laptop and a large monitor. Diana turned to take it all in. How come she'd never been here before?

The shopkeeper swatted at the surface of the desk. "Do take a seat. I'm sorry. Old Philbin needs to dust a bit more often."

He sat at the desk and bent to unlock a drawer. He pulled out a sturdy brown box and riffled the postcards inside.

"Each of these postcards has been selected to fit your criteria," he said. "They have postage dates between nineteen hundred and the late nineteen-thirties. Each of them was sent to an address in London. There are forty-three postcards in the box, and you need to select one of them." He looked up with a smile. "Who would like to pick one out?"

"Perhaps Zaf would do the honours?" suggested Robin. "I can see he's enjoying the aesthetic of the shop."

"Are you sure?" Zaf asked. "It feels like a lot of pressure."

Alexsei shrugged. "You can't get it wrong. There is no pressure."

Zaf took a chair in front of the desk, his gaze on the box. Diana wondered what he was thinking. Did Kamran know about his relationship with Alexsei?

"The decorative sides of the postcards are facing towards you," said the shopkeeper as he pushed the box towards Zaf. "You can't see the addresses. Pick one at random."

Zaf flicked through the pile.

As he did, a postcard in another box on a nearby shelf caught Diana's attention. The style and colouring was familiar, and with a start she realised that the little art nouveau fairy was very much like one that the mystery man had dropped when she'd bumped into him at the London Eye.

She reached over, careful not to be noticed, and pulled it out inside its protective cellophane pocket. She studied the back; the reverse was browning with age but unmarked.

Zaf pulled out a postcard from the box on the desk.

"You have made your selection?" said the shopkeeper.

Zaf nodded.

"In that case, would you like to read the address out for us, young sir? Come round here to announce it if you like."

Zaf stood and edged his way round to stand by the shop-keeper. He glanced around at everyone's faces. They all waited in silence.

"Durham Cathedral," said Robin, noting the picture on the front of the postcard.

Zaf cleared his throat. "So this postcard was sent by someone called John to his friend Mary in the year... actually, I can't read the postmark."

The shopkeeper leaned in. "The stamps show George the Fifth in profile, which puts it somewhere between nineteen-twelve and nineteen-thirty-four. It's a penny postage which excludes a brief three-year period after nineteen-eighteen when the price went up, however I believe that this postcard image was first made available in nineteen-fourteen." He nodded. "I would suggest that John sent this during the early part of the Great War."

Zaf looked at the shopkeeper, his face alight. "You're like the Sherlock Holmes of postcards."

The shopkeeper smiled. A cough from Kamran brought Zaf back to the task in hand.

"Sorry," he said." You're waiting for the address. It's forty-two Porter Road in West Kensington, London."

The players and assistants jabbed the address into their phones. The shopkeeper tapped it into his laptop. Diana leaned towards the monitor.

"Here's the map," said the shopkeeper. He zoomed in with his mouse and everyone leaned forward to look. "Hmmm."

"What?" snapped Kamran.

The shopkeeper looked up. "That's interesting. There is no longer a number forty-two."

Diana raised an eyebrow. *A puzzle.*

Alexsei looked at Robin. "Do we have... precedent for this?"

Robin shook her head. "No. It's up to each team to uncover the truth of where the target area might be, and then to make a purchase as close as possible to there. I will be the final judge."

"We're free to get on with it then?" said Zaf.

"You are all free to progress the task," Robin replied.

As they moved back through the shop, Diana lingered, the

vintage postcard in her hand. The shopkeeper noticed and gave her a smile.

"Ah, the beautiful Butterfly Girls. An artist named Schmucker created these in the very early twentieth century. There are six variants in total. I have been lucky enough to have a number of them in their original state, unused, unblemished."

"They're rare?"

"Uncommon. But popular. This postcard dates from 1907. If Old Philbin recalls correctly, Schmucker was afflicted with paralysis from childhood polio, which I think brings a certain poignancy to his art."

Diana fished around in her bag and pulled out the folded caricature she'd had drawn yesterday.

"Would this be one of your customers?" she asked.

Old Philbin squinted at the image. "Vernon Monroth. Yes, I know him. This isn't his sort of thing. Perhaps too kitsch for his tastes."

Diana tapped the paper. "But this man, this is that Vernon?"

"Monroth? Yes. He's an art dealer, or at least he was. His clients, and manners, have deteriorated over the years. He used to live on a houseboat at Chelsea, the *Fighting Temeraire,* he called it. Don't think he understood the irony of the name. But I hear he had to move it further east when he couldn't afford to moor it there."

"Eish!" called Errol from the front of the shop. "Have I lost my helper already?"

"Sorry!" Diana called back. She turned back to Old Philbin. "Thank you so much."

He gave her a shrug in response and she hurried to the

front of the shop, trying to focus her mind on the challenge ahead of her.

But she had a name. The drowned man, he had a name!

Vernon Monroth.

He was real, and she'd seen him. And if he had a name, then she might be able to discover more about him.

CHAPTER SIXTEEN

ZAF PHOTOGRAPHED the front and back of the postcard and memorised the address. No one had asked about the contents of the postcard, which was a shame, because it intrigued him. *Dear Mary, I expect to be home tomorrow. Yours, John.*

Was the post ever delivered that quickly?

Kamran clasped Zaf's shoulder to steer him out of the shop. "So, Zaf. What should our first move be?"

Zaf swallowed. Was this a test? Oxnard Pike had already spirited Alexsei away towards the far end of Cecil Court. *Gone.*

Zaf tried to focus on the matter in hand.

"Right," he said. "We need to find where the original building was so you can buy somewhere close to it. Let's start with some Googling."

"Then we shall do that in the car," said Kamran. "Quickly. I have a strategy that depends upon us being the first on site."

Zaf hurried to keep up as Kamran strode to a vehicle parked across the road. A man in overalls waited to hand them the keys.

"You will drive, yes?"

It took Zaf a moment to realise that Kamran was talking to him.

He hesitated. He hadn't driven in months, not since he'd left Birmingham. And this was a van. A proper, full-size white van.

It was huge.

"You can drive, surely?" Kamran said. "That was somewhat key to my strategy."

Zaf tried not to show how terrified he was. Driving a massive van, in London?

"I have passed my test," he said, "but I've never owned a car, and I've never driven in London. Not a car, and definitely not a van."

Kamran shrugged. "You will be fine. A good time to expand your skills. I will need you to go as quickly as possible, though."

Zaf climbed in and tried to fool himself into thinking this was normal. He'd put on his seatbelt, start the van, select a gear and drive off. Kamran had said he would be fine. He would be fine.

He pulled on the best smile he could muster, his heart thumping in his chest. *It'll be fine.*

The engine stalled.

Zaf turned the key again, like this was something he'd expected. He beamed at Kamran and the van started.

Phew.

Soon he was heading west along Crawford Street.

"See?" said Kamran. "You're doing great." He pointed ahead. "Turn right at these lights then take the first right."

Zaf swallowed. Right turns, in central London, in this van? He smiled nervously, careful not to take his eyes off the road.

"But now you have the hang of it," Alexsei's father added, "you can go a bit faster than ten miles per hour."

Zaf concentrated as he increased speed, although sustaining any kind of speed in London was a short-lived experience. He was starting to feel a little more at ease. It wasn't long before he was stationary again, waiting at traffic lights.

"So why are we in a van?" he asked.

"Aha. Let me tell you about my new strategy. Every year we have this same challenge, and nobody ever thought to do this. In the back of this van we have a number of estate agent signs. We arrive at Porter Road and we erect these signs. Guess who will answer the phone when our competitors call the number on the signs, trying to buy the property?"

Zaf clamped his tongue between his teeth as the lights turned green and they turned onto the A5. Kamran pointed out the right turn towards Hyde Park. There was no satnav in this van and he was reliant on Kamran to tell him where to go.

"Um," he said, "I'm not sure. Why do you want to... Oh, wait. It's me, isn't it? It'll be me who answers the phone."

Kamran roared with laughter. "I knew you were a good choice of helper. Yes, it will be you. We will slow down the opposition by wasting their time. It's good, no?"

Zaf nodded. It was certainly sneaky.

CHAPTER SEVENTEEN

DIANA AND ERROL VAN BLERK were in a printing shop on Charing Cross Road, nowhere near West Kensington. Diana still wasn't sure why there were here. Errol was all charm and smiles, but he had a level of focus that had seen him bundle Diana out of the door and down the street with barely a word.

"Apologies if I have been a little abrupt, Diana," he said, noticing the confusion on her face. "Speed is everything when it comes to this task."

"And you've struck me as a relaxed sort of man," she replied.

The South African stretched out his hands together and cracked his knuckles.

"I am a pleasure seeker. Pleasure seeker and leisure seeker. And there's nothing more fun than a jolly competition. I intend to win."

"And I'm here to help."

He nodded. "The sooner we can get along to Porter Road with the leaflets we're about to design, the better."

"I see," said Diana. "And what is the purpose of the leaflets?"

He turned to her, his eyes glittering with excitement. "I need to get as many homeowners as I can into a controlled environment. Controlled by me, that is. I will be offering them a free luxury mini-break in one of my finest hotels. I need to remove the possibility that they will engage with the other players."

Diana raised an eyebrow. "How will you target the leaflets if we don't know where number forty-two was?"

"My initial leaflet drop will be to all of the houses in the street. Do you think that will cover us?"

"What do you need me to do?"

He shrugged, amused. "What are you good at?"

"How about this," she said. "You work on your leaflet and I'll see what I can dig up about the history of the road. It would be unfortunate if the closest property was on a different road and you missed someone out from your leaflet drop."

"Good idea, girl. I will arrange for us both to have laptops. These people do a great deal of business for me and they will be happy to help."

Diana considered his plan as laptops and tea were brought to them. It would be useful to see a map of the area from the early twentieth century. She spent a few minutes on Google and soon she was gazing upon a view of Porter Road from the eighteen-nineties. She compared it side-by-side with the current street view.

"Well, I never."

Errol looked up, a question on his face.

"Give me one moment," Diana said. "I think I know what might have happened."

A few more searches confirmed her suspicion.

"Take a look at this." She pointed at the screen as Errol leaned in. "See here? This is the lower end of Porter Road in the eighteen-nineties. See how it's much longer? Here is that area now, replaced by a high-rise council estate. It was bombed during World War Two."

"So our target address is not even called Porter Road any longer?" Errol nodded, impressed. "Thank you for the heads-up. I will need to target different homeowners."

Twenty minutes later, he had a wad of invitations. They were printed on thick paper, with embossing, and looked credible. The two of them left the printers and climbed into the car outside.

"Do the rules allow you to have a driver?" she asked.

"Of course they do."

"Only I saw that Kamran got Zaf to drive. He didn't look all that happy about it."

Errol laughed. "I think Kamran wanted to get the measure of his young assistant. See what he's made of."

Diana nodded. She wondered if she was being tested too.

CHAPTER EIGHTEEN

ZAF TOOK the right turn Kamran indicated, then snaked his way through back roads towards the Bayswater Road. As they passed Hyde Park, Kamran pointed.

"Turn left, here!"

Zaf frowned. "We can't—"

"We can. Turn left, into the park. Short cut."

Zaf did as he was told, his hands tight on the steering wheel. Surely they were going to find themselves stuck in the park, driving along a pedestrian footpath?

But Kamran was right. There was a road cutting straight through the middle of Hyde Park that he'd somehow never known about. Minutes later they were in Kensington, closing in on their location.

As they approached Cromwell Road, his inner tourist guide (and that bit of him that wanted to impress his boyfriend's dad) couldn't resist pointing out the Victoria and Albert and the Natural History Museum, and dropping a few facts about each.

"The Natural History Museum. That is the one with the dinosaur skeleton?" said Kamran.

"Actually, Dippy the dinosaur is on tour at the moment," Zaf replied. "Pennsylvania, I believe. Hope the blue whale hangs in the museum's Hintze Hall for the time being."

"A dinosaur," muttered Kamran. "That would have been good for the Egg Sandwich challenge."

"Would it?" said Zaf, not understanding.

At last they reached Porter Street and Kamran bounded out of the van. "Come on, Zaf, we have signs to erect."

It didn't take long for Zaf to realise that putting up estate agent signs was physically quite demanding. He had a large rubber mallet to hammer them into the ground, but there wasn't much bare earth, which meant an additional challenge of finding a way to secure them. Worst of all was the speed with which Kamran wanted this done. Alexsei's father might have been a man with a plan, but he was happy for Zaf to do all the physical work.

Zaf sprinted up and down from the van, shoving signs into flower tubs and using cable ties to fasten them to railings. Most of the houses were the old three storey ones, not quite as grand as the one he and Diana lived in, but distinguished enough to be very expensive.

"Hey! What do you think you're doing?" said a woman emerging from one of the houses.

"Oh! Hi," said Zaf. "I was just erecting a sign for the estate agent."

Kamran had been watching from the van, but didn't take long to appear behind him.

"I am sorry," he said. "Has the young man put a sign in the wrong place?" He shook his head at Zaf.

The homeowner looked puzzled. "Yes. Yes, he has."

"Let me take care of that for you." Kamran gave an imperious wave of the hand, dismissing Zaf and the sign. "Away with the sign. Now, am I correct that you are the homeowner?"

"I am, yes." The woman narrowed her eyes.

Kamran smiled. "Fascinating property. Its proportions are very pleasing. The light falls well onto the windows, I think."

"Thank you," said the woman. "So what is it you're doing exactly?" She indicated the estate agents signs lined up along the road.

"Location scout for a TV company," Kamran replied.

She frowned. "Surely you don't actually buy property for that?"

"Ah," said Kamran, tapping the side of his nose. "It's a new series. We'll need a whole street of houses for years to come. Big budget stuff. Would you be open to a chat about your place?"

"I... I guess."

Kamran approached her front door. "Number thirty! I feel good about this address. Is it the highest number in the road?"

The woman nodded.

"Oh, can the lad come in to take notes?" Kamran asked.

Lad?

Zaf sighed and propped the sign against the railings, then followed Kamran inside.

CHAPTER NINETEEN

DIANA AND ERROL pulled into Porter Road and the driver parked behind a van. Was that the one Zaf and Kamran had left in?

"Hey, Diana, you see this?" said Errol, grinning. "See all these signs?"

There was a row of identical estate agent signs along the street. A middle-aged man with an enormous bushy moustache was wrestling one out of a planter, an angry scowl on his face.

"What do you make of them?" asked Errol.

"I suspect this is an attempt to de-rail us with some time-wasting. One of your friends could be behind this."

"That was my exact thinking. Let me tell you what would be fun. I am going to deliver these leaflets to the people in the flats at the end, and while I do that, I want you to call the number and pretend to play along."

"You do?"

"It will be hilarious. Follow me."

Diana phoned the number, making sure it was on loud-speaker so that Errol could hear.

"Hello?" came a voice.

"Hi, I'm interested in the house you have for sale on Porter Road," said Diana.

Errol gave her a thumbs-up.

"Yeah? Which one?" came the voice. "We have a number of properties in, er, that part of town."

"Number twenty, what's the asking price?"

"Yes, we have had a lot of interest in that property," said the voice. "So much interest."

Diana couldn't resist a smile at Errol. "Yes, but what's the asking price?"

"The asking price? Right, yes. Well, it's more of a guide really but—"

Diana stopped walking. She knew that voice. "Zaf, is that you?"

"Diana? Oh."

Diana shook her head and ended the call. She didn't like being pitted against her friend and co-worker.

Errol pulled a face. "Eish, you blew it, Di!"

"My integrity is not a part of this deal."

"What are you talking about?"

"I have no interest in tormenting good people for your amusement."

Errol held up his hands in defence. "I didn't realise that you weren't up for a bit of fun! Who are we tormenting?"

"You've got Zaf pretending to be an estate agent, me pretending to be a buyer—"

"It's a game! I picked you because I thought you might be a bit more relaxed about these things. Kids these days, they're so serious. Like po-faced bloody missionaries. Can't have no fun these days without offending someone."

Diana pulled in a breath. "I'm sorry. This is a game. I get it."

"Exactly. And you're paid to help us have fun, aren't you?"

"Yes. I am." He was right, however she felt about it. And maybe he had a point.

"Good. Errol gave her a smile. "Now, help me post these leaflets."

CHAPTER TWENTY

Kamran had agreed with the woman to buy her house. Simple as that. Whether she bought his story about needing houses for a TV series didn't matter. He mentioned some numbers, added a little, and eventually she said yes.

The amount of money involved boggled Zaf's mind. If he worked for a hundred years as a tour guide and got to keep all of the money, he'd just about be able to buy this house. And Kamran had bought it to win a game. He was on the phone to a solicitor who'd progress the sale, but the agreement was there.

Zaf made his way back along the road, collecting the signs. Most of them had been ripped up and tossed into the gutter. He put them back into the van.

"Is that it?" he said, tossing the last sign into the van,

Kamran consulted his watch. "Not even lunchtime and we're done. A good day's work, Zaf, my man. We should go back to Errol's little backstreet spa and wait for the others to complete."

Zaf closed the rear doors of the van. "I thought the challenge would take up the whole day."

Kamran shook his head. "The Tradition. It's not about the games."

"Isn't it?"

Kamran gave him a sideways look. "OK, maybe it is a little. I have spent more time thinking about these challenges than I will ever spend competing in them. But I'm a planner. You know my son, Alexsei, right? He's your landlord, yes?"

Zaf felt his skin prickle. *More than my landlord.* He nodded.

"He tell you what business I'm in?"

"Oil, isn't it?"

Kamran scoffed. "Oil. The word covers a multitude of businesses. And sins. You're driving us back, yes?"

"Yes."

The two of them got into the van's cab. Kamran turned in his seat to address Zaf.

"My father worked for the Azerbaijan state oil company. He saw the future and, even though Azerbaijan was part of the Soviet Union and it was the height of the Cold War, he made sure I had the best education possible. So he sent me here to London to be educated at St Julian's. I returned home, with a degree in Chemical Engineering from Stockholm and my position in the state company assured. The collapse of communism was a... profitable moment for our family and I worked hard to build my own skills and my own businesses."

"So, not just oil?"

Kamran shrugged. "Drilling, mining, transportation, exploration. You know what all these things have in common, Zaf?"

"Big machines?"

"Planning! They are all feats of planning. Let Oxnard buy works of art on impulsive whims. Let Errol go where his sense of pleasure takes him. Me, I am a planner. I have my life already entirely planned out. And my son's life. And his sons' lives."

Zaf stared out of the windscreen. Alexsei's life, planned out by his father. Did he know?

Kamran laughed. "I have made plans to help me win these challenges for a very long time. You know that, Robin." He looked down, glancing at the bodycam pinned to his lapel, then turned to Zaf. "But these days in London, they serve a higher function."

"What's that?" asked Zaf.

"It's an excuse for three busy men to spend time together. Old friends. Good friends. The Tradition is the one thing that draws us back together. Without it, we might only see each other again at each other's funerals."

Zaf nodded. He didn't see his own old friends often enough. Since leaving Birmingham for uni, he'd only been home twice. Maybe he should visit his family, introduce them to Alexsei.

"Right, so we go back now." Karman buckled his seat belt. "Drive on."

The route back to the spa on Manchester Street took them along Holland Park Avenue and through Notting Hill.

"And what kind of a man was your friend, Tristram?" said Zaf. "If you don't mind me asking."

Kamran frowned, then angled his head so he could be heard by the bodycam microphone. "He was the best of us," he said, then looked at Zaf. "He was all things. Given the chance, he would have lived all our lives a thousand times over. There was no business venture he would not consider. He had us all working together in his final years."

"That's nice."

Kamran was silent. Zaf waited, wondering if he'd put his foot in it.

At last the older man continued. "London's freeport. Or what was going to be the freeport. You know what those are, Zaf?"

"I don't think I do."

Kamran smiled. He seemed to enjoy finding things Zaf didn't know. "Imagine you import goods into this country. You pay taxes, duty."

"OK, yes."

"So, the goods arrive and the more they're worth, the more tax you pay, yes?"

"Yes."

"But you don't pay the taxes as soon as they arrive. They have to be processed."

Zaf nodded. "Like when you go through customs. *Anything to declare.*"

"Precisely. So there is a time and a place where goods are in a country but the owners have not yet had to pay taxes on them."

"OK..."

"So, if you had goods that you want to be in a country but not actually 'in' a country, you could save yourselves millions of pounds by keeping them in that in-between place. Here but not here."

Zaf frowned. "I *think* I understand."

"That is a freeport. You can store things there, even manufacture them there and not be subject to the tax laws of the land. It encourages business. It is a good thing. And there was to be a freeport in London, not far from Tilbury Docks. Tristram was constructing a secure storage facility there. Well, it was Errol's company doing the construction. My team offered some engineering and security expertise. All of us, working on a project together."

"And Oxnard... I mean, Mr Pike?"

Kamran laughed again. It was as if he allowed himself several loud laughs a day, as a counterpoint to the seriousness.

"Oxnard needed somewhere to store his extensive private art collection, away from the eyes of the taxman. Being Tristram's most illustrious patron was his contribution. You would not believe the masterpieces that man owns."

Zaf nodded, still unsure what he made of the relationship between the men.

"Come," said Kamran. "Let's drive."

As they headed back, Zaf felt a little more confident than he had that morning. He parked on Manchester Street.

"We can't park here for long," he said.

Kamran patted him on the shoulder. "What will the police and traffic wardens do? Give me a ticket? Tow it away? Do you think I need to keep this van?"

Zaf shrugged. The casualness of it all...

He followed Kamran inside, to find the efficient Mindy waiting. She escorted them to a room where Robin Silversmith was monitoring the bodycam feeds on a bank of monitors. Zaf had forgotten about his, but now he looked forward to removing it.

"You have finished for the day?" Robin asked. "Your participation in the task is complete?"

"Yes," said Kamran.

"Very good. Then you are welcome to join me here and see how your colleagues are doing."

Zaf slid into a chair and looked around.

He suspected the room was usually some sort of therapy spa room. The floor was tiled, the walls papered in an olive green and the furnishings mildly clinical.

He moved his chair to see the screen. Each participant had a dedicated monitor. His and Kamran's were now dark as they'd removed their bodycams, but he could still see the feeds from Errol, Diana, Oxnard and Alexsei.

Diana and Errol were in a tower block, which intrigued him. Zaf had noticed a council estate nearby, but it wasn't even on Porter Road.

He turned to Oxnard and Alexsei's feeds. Oxnard seemed to be showing a young couple pictures on a tablet.

"What are they doing?" he asked Robin.

Robin reclined in her chair. "I believe that Oxnard is attempting the 'house swap' move. He has a desirable property in the country somewhere. Obviously, a man like Oxnard has them everywhere, from Brooke Mansion on Hampstead Lane to the villa in the Scilly Isles. Ideally it should be worth around one and a half times the value of the property that he's attempting to buy, so that it presents an unmissable opportunity to the target. His main job is trying not to look like a scammer. He may have called on one of his celebrity friends to act as a character witness." She gave a small laugh. "Classic Oxnard."

Zaf watched as Oxnard continued his show and tell.

"This couple has a young family," said Robin. "I imagine Oxnard's pitch is leaning hard on the local schools and the wholesome countryside."

Eventually, the couple agreed to the sale, and they shook hands. The deal was done.

"What was Alexsei's part in all of that?" asked Zaf.

Robin glanced at Zaf. "As far as I could tell, he carried Oxnard's briefcase."

Zaf winced. *Dull.* At least Kamran had given him plenty to do.

CHAPTER TWENTY-ONE

DIANA AND ERROL had spent an hour or so delivering leaflets to the flats in the tower block. The lift was broken in the next block over and they found themselves behind a man struggling up the stairs, hauling a tartan shopping trolley.

Wheezing, the man paused at the sixth floor.

"Are you alright?" asked Diana.

The old fellow waved a hand at her. "I'm grand. I'll be wanting a cup of tea when I'm done, mind."

Diana put a hand on the trolley. "Let me help you with that."

The man smiled his thanks.

Errol had overtaken and was on the seventh floor. He leaned over the railing to call down. "Diana. We must proceed."

"You go ahead," she called. "I'll not be long."

"Dearie me," said the man with the trolley. "I'll not be the cause of strife."

"Nearly all of my strife is of my own making," Diana told him, pulling the trolley up the stairs.

"What's the story with you two then?" asked the man.

"He needs to buy a flat and he's running out of time."

"He not got anywhere to live?"

"It's a sort of a, er, target he has to hit." Diana wasn't about to describe the purchase of pricey London property as a game.

"Looking for a flat then. You'll have seen number seventy-five? For sale with Hazells? Shockingly overpriced, if you ask me."

They reached the eighth floor to find Errol shoving leaflets through letter boxes.

Diana turned to the man. "Is this your floor?"

"Oh no." The man gave her an apologetic smile. "I'm another three up."

"Not a problem."

When she'd delivered the man's trolley safely to his floor, she made her way down to rejoin Errol, calling the estate agent as she went. Errol was on the ninth floor now, his body language cold.

Diana held out her phone. He stared at it, his tanned face creased with a frown.

"The estate agent," she said. "A real one. Number seventy-five is for sale."

He made the call, his eyes on her face as he spoke. His expression was neutral, almost unreadable.

"I need to go to the estate agents to sign the paperwork," he said after ending the call.

"Excellent news," Diana replied. "Are we going there now?"

"Oh, you're coming with me?"

"Of course."

"I wasn't sure if you were a team player." He slapped the

phone into her hand and made for the stairs. She followed in silence. She wasn't about to let this man get to her.

Outside the block, he turned to her, only mildly out of breath.

"Do you know how important these challenges are?" he said.

"I thought it was all about the fun for you, Mr van Blerk."

"It is. It is all about fun and pleasure. There's a pleasure in winning, you know?"

"I see." She gave him a smile. Errol van Blerk wasn't a man who appealed to her, but he was a client.

Their driver was waiting at the car, the back door already open. Errol stepped inside and Diana followed. Errol gave him an address then leaned back in the soft leather seat.

"I don't want to be that guy," he said.

"Sorry," said Diana, "what guy?"

"The guy who says *jump* and you say *how high?*"

"No. I'm sure you don't."

"But..."

She waited.

He looked at her, his brow furrowed. "All I suggested was a harmless jape where you misled Kamran's pretend estate agent, but you bailed at the first sentence."

"It didn't sit right with me."

"And then, in the middle of a critical mission, you stopped to help some old man with his stupid trolley."

She bristled. "I can't help wanting to help others."

"You think I don't help people?" said Errol, fingers splayed across his own chest.

Diana met his gaze. "I don't know, Mr van Blerk."

"Ah, knock it off with the *Mr van Blerk*. I know you

English. You hide all your snide attitudes behind a veil of politeness."

Diana took a breath. He was a client. Whatever she thought about him...

"I'm sorry," she said. "Errol."

He huffed and looked out the window.

"If you don't mind me reminding you," she said, "it was because I was talking to that man that we knew number seventy-five was for sale."

"Which is why I'm talking to you here and not watching you disappear in the rear view mirror back there." His expression was pinched. "You know the phrase, *work hard, play hard?*"

"Yes."

"That's me. I'm driven by the quest for pleasure, but I am driven. My construction companies are the hardest working in the world. My hotel in Abu Dhabi. Six-star hotel. Thirty floors. My team had it up in just over two years. Do we sail close to the wind? Do we bend certain rules and restrictions? Sure. But we get the job done. And those lads are all well paid." He gestured into the distance. "My hotel resorts in Borneo. I gave them millions more to protect habitats for the orangutans. I did that."

"That's very noble."

He glared at her as if to check for sarcasm.

"That feller with the trolley," he said. "I could give him a thousand quid. I could pay to have their lift repaired."

"I'm sure you could," Diana replied with a smile.

"But I don't let petty concerns interfere with my game."

"I understand."

"Good." He went back to looking out of the window.

"May I offer a thought?" Diana said.

"It's a free country."

"I don't think I ever separate my working life and my personal life."

"How's that?"

Diana considered. "I treat people in my work life the same way I treat people in my personal life. I am the same person. It's like... if I may make a confession...?"

Errol turned to her. "I like a good confession."

She nodded. "Yesterday, the tickets for the London Eye I'd been given... they turned out to be duds."

"Fakes?"

She tilted her head. "From a less than reputable source. We were going to fail you. I had to run to the ticket office and I was stuck in the queue and then... I saw an old friend." Her mouth twitched involuntarily. "Sort of an old friend. Ariadne Webb. We go way back but we both ended up in the tour guide business. She works for this company ACE Tours. Authentic Customer Experiences. I saw her and she offered to help us out with fresh tickets."

"Is that so?"

"She and I both know the value of building up friendships. Connections and contacts. A kind word here or there pays dividends in the long run."

"You think I don't know how to grease the wheels of business?"

"I don't think it's about greasing the wheels, if it's a natural part of your behaviour."

Diana leaned back. Was she telling him too much? But she'd never meet this man again, after this week.

"Maybe Ariadne is a little bit more cynical and calculating

about it," she said. "She can turn on the charm if she knows she'll get something out of it." Diana smiled at her memories of Ariadne. "And she'd have *loved* to wind up the competition. Zero qualms about leading 'estate agent' Zaf on a merry dance. But the point is, I'll always reach out a hand to help others because I've made it part of my nature."

Errol was nodding. "You're a woman of principle."

"I prefer to think I'm pathologically nice."

He grinned. "I believe you are, Diana."

After visiting the estate agent, they returned to Errol's spa on Manchester Street, the atmosphere between them far more amicable than it had been in the tower block. Zaf was already at the spa, in a white and green room that had been transformed into a control and observation centre.

Robin Silversmith was at a bank of screens. She turned to Diana. "Is your task for the day complete?"

"It is," replied Diana.

"Very well. You can watch."

Diana slumped into a seat beside Zaf. All those stairs had taken their toll on her thighs.

Zaf leaned over to whisper to her. "I think everyone's bought a place by now. Can you believe it? The moneythey've spent."

Diana raised her eyebrows. "They all really want to win."

Robin was listening in. "Winning is everything to them. None of them would deny it."

"Millions of pounds have been thrown at this game today," said Zaf. "And it's not even four o'clock."

"And how does that make you feel?" Robin asked, her gaze on the screens.

"Feel?" said Zaf. He frowned. "Honestly?"

"Honestly," replied Robin. She was editing the footage on the screens.

"A little bit sick," Zaf said. "It's been fun. But, that kind of wealth. I mean, I can't even scrape together the deposit for a bedsit. Seeing that amount of cash thrown about... Yeah, it makes me uneasy."

CHAPTER TWENTY-TWO

It was late afternoon by the time Oxnard Pike and Alexsei returned to rejoin the rest of the party in the spa's beautiful roof garden. Many cups of tea had been drunk and numerous pastries nibbled.

Now, while the three competitors and three helpers waited, Robin pored over the legal documents that had been presented as evidence. She had her own reference documents, and made a number of calls to consult people who were apparently conducting additional research for her.

A member of the spa's waiting staff wheeled in a trolley laden with little plates of salmon blinis and several bottles of champagne in a bucket. Robin waited until everyone was settled with a glass of fizz before beginning her announcement.

"Let us begin," she said. "There is champagne for us to toast the winner, and of course, you will *all* toast each other as worthy competitors. Let me show you my conclusions."

The champagne was Krug, non-vintage, Diana noted. The good stuff.

Robin pressed a button and a display screen placed against a vine-covered trellis came to life with a single image.

"Here we have Porter Road, the subject of today's task. As we observed at the beginning of the day, number forty-two no longer exists. I believe only one of our teams uncovered the correct reason for this."

She nodded towards Diana and Errol and switched the display to a street plan. "You will see how the modern street is truncated at the bottom, compared with some of the neighbouring streets. If we look at a much older version, it's a different story."

Robin pressed a key and the older view was overlaid on the modern map, showing a street that extended much further.

"See how the lower part has gone? Let me show you a map of bombing intensity from the Blitz in World War Two, and that will explain where those houses went. In the post-war years, the council built a housing estate there, so the location of our address was actually in the area now occupied by Chesterfield House, a block of flats."

There was muttering among the men. Errol beamed, while Kamran and Oxnard looked frustrated.

"Back to the modern-day view," said Robin. "The red dot on the screen shows the location of our target address. I am satisfied with the quality and legal standing of the agreements that you have all made today, so I will now show the properties that you have purchased on this view." She pressed the button and three more dots appeared, marked in blue. "Here is Mr van Blerk's purchase, here is Mr Dadashov's, and here is Mr Pike's."

Errol punched the air and whooped. His purchase, in the tower block, was visibly closer to the target than the others.

Robin held up a hand to silence him. "However, there is more to this."

"What?" said Errol. "What more can there be? Mine is closest, see?"

"I shall switch to a 3D view," said Robin. "We know from the historical records, that number forty-two Porter Road was a house in the same style as the ones that remain, so it would have appeared very much as this wireframe view indicates."

The view swivelled, showing how the buildings would have looked from street level. The ghostly shape of number forty-two was much lower than the modern-day tower block that stood in its place.

"Now, I will show Errol's purchase from this angle. See how high up it is? Much higher than the house would have been. If we measure the distance from the original roofline of number forty-two, Errol's flat is further away by around two metres than Kamran's house."

Errol roared with rage. "We've never worked in three dimensions before! How do you even know the distance? Did you measure it?"

"I am a competent judge, Mr van Blerk."

"This is discrimination!"

Robin stepped away from her keyboard and regarded them all silently.

"Are you accusing me of dishonesty, Errol? Are you saying I am a cheat?"

Errol waved at the screen. "But it's obvious. We've never used three dimensions before."

"I shall repeat myself," said Robin. "Do you think I have deliberately cheated you?"

Her stare met his.

"No, no, of course not," he seethed, looking at the ground. "Obviously, we all trust your judgement."

"Quite right," she said. "I used hard facts and a little mathematics. I made sure that my work was checked by competent people and I stand by my decision. All of my workings are available to view, everything is completely transparent."

"But three dimensions... That's a new rule."

Robin gave him a smile. "You all charged me with providing the final adjudication. I have used my judgement, and you must live with it. Kamran wins."

Errol's mouth was working, like he was chewing on something. "Congratulations, Kamran," he said at last, forcing a smile. He shook his head, and then his smile grew. "You beat me, old friend. Well done."

Everyone joined in with a toast to the winner. Zaf, as Kamran's assistant, got his own toast, and then everyone else was congratulated for completing the task.

"Dinner is at eight," said Robin. "Your time is your own for now."

Errol left the roof garden to 'attend to business matters'. Kamran and Oxnard decided to finish the champagne and Kamran insisted his son stay to recount his part in Oxnard's venture.

Diana leaned over to Zaf. "I thought I might take a walk round to the depot and see that everything is in order."

She hoped he would pick up on the implied suggestion that he join her.

He turned to her, nodding. "I'll join you if that's alright?"

CHAPTER TWENTY-THREE

ZAF AND DIANA walked the short distance to Chiltern Street. The Serenity Haven and the bus depot almost backed onto one another, except for the road that ran between them.

"Is that what old people friendships are like?" said Zaf, jerking a thumb back towards the spa.

"Old people?" said Diana. "They're all younger than me, Zaf."

"OK. *Adult* friendships. They only meet up once a year and they use that time to score points against each other. Is that friendship?"

"Old friendships are either hard to maintain, or held together by what little people have in common. We grow and change. The friends we have are not necessarily the friends we'd choose if we'd met them for the first time now."

He shook his head. It didn't make sense to him. Staying in touch with people for so many years, then spending their time together racing around the city, competing.

"Huh. We shouldn't waste energy on people who aren't good for us."

Diana smiled. "You're still finding new friends round every corner. Those men back here, they've got history together. And a shared tragedy."

He nodded. "Do you know how Tristram Ramsgate died?"

She shook her head.

"Alexsei told me. This stuff called halon gas. I had to look it up. It's used as a fire suppressant in places where there are important objects to protect and no humans."

"It pushes out the oxygen so the fire goes out. I know it."

"Tristram was in a secure facility he owned out west along the Thames. The fire alarm went off when he was inside and..."

Diana winced. "Asphyxiation. Not nice."

Yeah, he thought, trying not to imagine it. "They all worked on this place, the freeport. All of the men contributed to its construction. Well, I think Oxnard was aiming to be its first customer."

They were at the depot now. The sun was setting over Chiltern Street and it looked like a painting. They stopped at the door-within-a-door leading inside.

"I Googled Tristram Ramsgate's death," Diana said. "The inquest said death by misadventure."

Zaf frowned and held the door open for her. Newton Crombie was in the depot, finishing up his cleaning and maintenance routine.

"Missed us?" asked Zaf.

Newton looked up. "Been out having fun?"

"Something like that." He continued through to the little kitchen to put the kettle on.

Over a cup of tea and a custard cream, Diana gave an overview of the day. Newton was most interested in the part where they described how Robin used a 3D model of the house to make height comparisons.

"What software did she use?" he asked.

Zaf looked at Diana. They both shrugged.

"No idea," Zaf said.

"Oh, OK." Newton looked wistful. Zaf could imagine 3D computer modelling of London buildings being his thing.

He realised that they hadn't been joined by the depot cat, butting his head against their legs and hassling them for crumbs of biscuit.

"Where's Gus?" he asked.

Diana looked up from her mug of tea, frowning.

"He's taken to sneaking into the cupboards," said Newton. "He loves a secret space."

"Don't we all?" Diana said.

Newton sighed. "The funny thing is that sometimes I swear I see him go into one cupboard and come out of a different one."

Zaf smiled. That sounded like regular Gus behaviour. The cat had a habit of turning up all over the place.

Right on cue, there was a small trilling sound from the cupboard where they kept the kitchen cleaning equipment. The door opened and Gus's face appeared. He strolled towards them, his tail high.

"I bet he's knocked over all the brooms," said Diana.

He made his way around all three of them, nudging their hands and making sure they all tickled his ears.

Diana went over to shut the door. There was a rumbling sound followed by a crash.

Zaf looked up from Gus, who he'd been tickling under the chin. "What?"

Diana was standing over a pile of shoes that had slid out of the cupboard. "Um. What is this?"

Zaf stared at the shoe pile, and at Gus who was busy washing himself, pretending not to see.

"Why are there so many women's shoes in here?" Diana asked.

Zaf and Newton both stood and went to the cupboard. Zaf leaned inside.

"Check this out," he said, pointing.

Newton leaned past him and prodded the back of the cupboard. It was made of thin board, not fastened properly to the sides. "I think he's been coming and going from the back."

Zaf knelt down and stuck his head and shoulders into the space. "There's a massive gap at the back."

He put his hand through into the space, expecting to feel the rough brickwork of the wall behind, and possibly the floor below. But the void was large, definitely big enough for Gus to use as part of a network of secret passages.

Zaf climbed out again. Diana was sifting through the shoes.

"There are some expensive shoes here. I can't believe how many he's brought back. Wherever he got that Louboutin from the other day, he's gone and got more."

Newton stared at the pile. "There's got to be thirty or fifty shoes here. And no pairs at all."

He was right. They were all single shoes.

"They're different sizes," said Newton. "The other ones were too."

"The other ones?" asked Diana.

Newton didn't answer but started to line them up in size order, grouping them by colour where he could. "Thirty-eight shoes, ranging from size three to size eight, but all ladies'."

"We need to put them all out of sight before Paul Kensington sees them," said Diana. "He doesn't need much of an excuse to lose his temper at Gus."

Newton pulled a face that said Paul Kensington would not be able to remove Gus without first removing Newton.

"Fine," he said. "I will tidy them away and try to find out where they came from. Not because of Paul Kensington, but because it's the right thing to do."

Zaf heard a trilling from behind him and turned to see Gus standing on the chair he'd been sitting in, reaching up for a custard cream.

"Oi!" he hissed. Gus jumped down and disappeared into another cupboard. Zaf slid back into his seat, eyeing the shoes.

"This isn't about to be the start of a Newton Crombie collection of shoes, is it?" said Diana. "That way lies madness."

Newton twitched his nose. "They hardly have the same appeal as a fine vehicle or a work of civil engineering." He stood, shoes gathered in his arms. "By the way, what did you say to him the other day?"

"Who?" Diana asked.

"Paul Kensington. He was really moody after you went in to talk to him."

"Ah, yes. He sourced some bogus tickets for the London Eye. It very nearly made things awkward with our guests, but I was able to rectify the situation. With some help."

Was she blushing?

"Good grief," said Newton. "Did he learn nothing from the Morris Walker debacle?" He wandered off shaking his head, arms laden with high class women's shoes.

Zaf looked at Diana over his mug of tea. "Don't you think it's time someone told me about the whole Morris Walker thing?"

"It's before your time, Zaf."

"And yet I think I'm the only person who's in the dark about that story. It's clearly had a big impact on this place."

Diana sighed. "Yes. Maybe it is time to tell you."

CHAPTER TWENTY-FOUR

Diana looked back at Zaf. He was right; he deserved to know about Morris Walker.

She licked her lips. "Morris Walker was the old boss of Chartwell and Crouch, years back, and he was a great boss. He knew how to get the best out of people and he knew the ins and outs of running a business. I'd worked with him before, back when he was a record producer."

Zaf opened his mouth to speak, then closed it.

Diana eyed him. "You read something in my diary, didn't you?"

He frowned and didn't meet her eye.

She felt her jaw clench. "I know you looked at my diaries. How else would you think to invite Pascal Palmer to my birthday the other month?"

"Um, yes." He looked up at her, his expression sheepish. "I read that you were a backing singer on a hit record in the eighties?"

"*Count Me In?*" Diana smiled. "Yes. It was a huge hit that one summer. You heard it everywhere. Morris had such a knack for tapping into the zeitgeist."

Zaf nodded.

Diana rolled her eyes. "I'd have loved to be a pop star, but... It was the era of the one hit wonder, and a woman has to put food on her table. Morris moved from music to tourism and brought me on board." She drew in a breath. "I think you already know that Ariadne Webb was also a singer on that track. She went to ACE Tours. We've had parallel careers of a sort. She split from Pascal Palmer twenty years ago. As you know, I stayed in touch with him for a while."

Diana didn't tell Zaf that Pascal had been in touch a couple of times since the barbecue birthday party.

"Back to the Chartwell and Crouch story," she continued. "A few years ago, a scandal came out of nowhere. Chartwell and Crouch were selling cut-price tickets for tours and events through a website. Thousands of them. West End shows, Madame Tussaud's, tours up and down the Thames. Except the tickets were worthless."

"What d'you mean?" asked Zaf.

"I mean they weren't proper tickets. It was fraud, and not even a very clever fraud. Just a website that promised things and then didn't deliver them."

"And this was Morris Walker's doing?"

Diana shrugged and then reluctantly nodded. "Morris denied everything. But he was in charge."

Zaf shook his head. "But surely the website could have been a spoof?"

"A joke?"

"A fake website, set up by someone else. A scam."

"I'm certain it was," said Diana. "I *was* certain it was. Morris was a trusted figure in my life, a friend. He believed in giving visitors to London the best possible value. It just wasn't in his nature... but there was a ton of evidence that pointed to Morris having set it up. The money went straight into an account in his name. He was convicted of fraud."

"He's in jail?"

She nodded. "They never found the money, so they threw the book at him. He's in Wandsworth jail. A seven-year sentence."

"Wow," said Zaf. "Oh wait, is this why Paul Kensington's always going on about money?"

"Absolutely. Morris never returned the funds. The company was obliged to make payouts of hundreds of thousands of pounds. And after everything that happened, he's probably under extra financial scrutiny. I'm not sure it explains everything about Paul Kensington, though."

Zaf smiled. "It's like he brings his own special grubby magic to the role. I wonder what it's like to work for a good boss? I can't even imagine."

Diana gave a small bark of laughter. "Well the ironic thing is that ACE tours where Ariadne works... they have a good manager, Tom Griffin. It's one reason they're doing better than us."

Zaf pursed his lips. "I don't know how I'm supposed to feel about ACE tours. They are our evil competitors, so I'm sure I should hate them."

She laughed. "They're not evil. Ariadne and I have... history. But the company has its act together in a way we don't." She sniffed. "It's annoying."

"Why?"

Diana let out a long, heartfelt sigh. "It's annoying that Paul Kensington just lazily steals their tour ideas in a half-baked way rather than figuring out what they're doing well and making improvements. It's annoying that they want to deliver decent tours showcasing the best that London has to offer, whereas we're being constantly hounded about cost cutting and utilisation rates." She looked at her watch. "We have dinner with our wealthy patrons in an hour and a bit. You might want to not fill up on custard creams."

Zaf paused, yet another biscuit halfway to his mouth. He looked at it and shrugged.

"I don't care if they've got lobster and caviar," he said. "You can't beat a custard cream."

CHAPTER TWENTY-FIVE

Zaf tore himself away from the biscuits and went to find Newton, who was busy sorting through the mountain of shoes. He'd lined up cardboard boxes on an ancient work bench and was examining each shoe in turn.

"What are you doing?" Zaf asked.

Newton glanced up. "Shoe triage."

"Can I help?"

Newton raised an eyebrow. "I suppose so. Grab a shoe and process it as follows." He swivelled the laptop towards Zaf. "First of all, see this list? This is all the luxury shoe brands whose shops are within a couple of miles of here. If you find a shoe that looks like it could pass for new and is one of these brands, then it goes in this box here."

"Right, got it."

"Then the next three boxes are for shoes that look nearly new, shoes that are very lightly scuffed and shoes that are quite well worn."

Zaf took a shoe from a box and looked at the brand. "Ooh, this is Dior! I think it could pass for new."

"In that box." Newton pointed. "There's a shop on Sloane Street."

Zaf processed more of the shoes along with Newton, who was totally absorbed by the task. They quickly triaged all of the shoes and Newton nodded.

"Right. Next phase. We put away the well-worn and lightly scuffed boxes and see if we can't move some of these others along."

Newton consulted the screen. "Our best bet is to go over to Harrods. They stock several of these brands. We can re-home eight of these shoes if we go there." He pulled out the eight shoes and put them into a Tesco carrier bag.

Zaf held up a hand. "Hold on a second. What is it we're planning to do, exactly?"

Newton huffed with irritation. "We're putting the shoes on the racks in the correct part of the Harrods shoe department."

"Why? We don't think the shoes came from there, do we?"

Newton made a seesaw motion with his hand. "Probably not. It seems a bit far for Gus to be making regular trips. It makes sense though, because the shoes will be in a place they belong."

"Newton, these are *shoes*. They're not social creatures. They don't flock together. Why does this seem like a good idea to you?"

Newton tapped his cheek as he searched for the words. "It's like putting the cutlery back in the right slot in the cutlery drawer in the kitchen. We are taking chaos and making it orderly."

"Wait, there's a system in that drawer?" Zaf asked.

"I knew it! You're the one who just throws things in there willy-nilly, aren't you?"

"Joking!" said Zaf hastily. He'd never knowingly put

anything away in the drawer, but wasn't going to confess to that. "And you're really going to do this?"

Newton gave him a disbelieving look. "Harrods is open until nine. If we're swift, we can do it now."

"Er..." Zaf looked round and was relieved to see Diana standing at the door to the depot, giving him a meaningful look. "Sadly, I have to go join our clients for dinner. This..." He waved a hand at the shoes. "I will leave this to you."

Gus sat on the end of the workbench, cleaning his paws with his pink raspy tongue.

"This is all your fault," Zaf muttered to him as he left.

At eight o'clock, he and Diana sat down with the five others in one of the Serenity Haven spa's spacious dining rooms. The table was laid with polished silver cutlery and large crystal wine glasses but that didn't detract from the minimalist tone of the spa.

Robin sat at the head of the table, reinforcing her position as judge. Zaf and Diana were at the foot of the table, alongside Alexsei. Was there a gap between the setting for the players and their helpers?

The starters were brought in: Asian salads of crunchy greens, slivers of fresh mango, and the subtle heat of ginger dressing. No choices were offered, and none requested. The only drink presented was water.

Errol saw Zaf looking at his glass.

"Kaapvaal glacial ice," he said, grinning. "Deep core. The ice in your glass is over eight hundred thousand years old."

"Old ice," said Zaf. "Sure it's okay to drink? T-Rexes didn't paddle in it or anything?"

Kamran gave one of his barks of laughter.

"Purer than any natural ice today," said Errol. "At two hundred pounds a cube, it ought to be."

Zaf nearly spat out at least fifty quid's worth of ancient water.

"But does it taste any different?" said Kamran. "Chemically, is it distinguishable from, say, Evian?"

Oxnard wagged a finger at him. "Content is not the mark of value. A thing is worth exactly what people think it's worth."

Over the starter, Oxnard quizzed Alexsei on his own work and affairs. Alexsei was seemingly happy to be seen as his father's proxy landlord in London and when Oxnard accused him of being a dilettante, Alexsei just shrugged.

"I'm happy listening to music, exploring London's culture and arts." He looked at Zaf as he spoke. Was he about to tell them?

"Surely you approve of my son's artistic temperament?" Kamran said to Oxnard. "Your whole livelihood is based around art."

"Ah, but who would be an artist?" said the Brit. "It's a fool's game. Gallery owners are rich. Art collectors are rich. But the artist? There are no rich artists."

"Damien Hurst, Anish Kapoor, Bridget Riley..." said Alexsei, ticking the names off on his fingers.

Oxnard waved a hand as though such 'facts' did not need countering.

"My son will move into the family business when the time is right," said Kamran.

Zaf looked at his boyfriend. It was like his whole life was planned to the day. Would Zaf only get to enjoy Alexsei's company until it was time to 'grow up'?

"Until that time..." Karma continued, "he is free to play as he wishes."

Errol laughed. "I've already got adult children – at least some boys and girls claiming to be mine – trying to worm their way into my wallet. Scroungers the lot of them."

"Life is full enough without offspring," said Oxnard.

Zaf could feel Diana listening attentively next to him. He wondered what she was making of all this.

Plates from the starters were whisked away and replaced with a main course of grilled salmon fillet with roasted vegetables. Zaf tasted a delicious drizzle of citrus-infused olive oil.

Robin, who'd barely eaten, put her fork aside. She clasped her hands together.

"Perhaps now, gentlemen, I should tell you a little about the task we must undertake on day two."

CHAPTER TWENTY-SIX

DIANA WATCHED the group turn its attention to the former valet sitting at the head of the table.

"It's the Sandwich Challenge tomorrow," said Oxnard. "We know that."

"You know the basics, Mr Pike." Robin surveyed the group. "It is a very simple task. You must eat an egg sandwich."

Zaf smiled. "That sounds simple."

"The challenge is that you must eat it in the most unusual place possible, within London."

Diana's mind was racing. "Can you define unusual?"

Oxnard threw out a hand. "In the pantry at Number Ten. On top of the Millennium Dome. In the storeroom of unwanted mannequins at Madame Tussauds. Unusual. What we need to know is, what is this year's twist?"

"Well, if you stop talking," said Errol, "we might actually hear it, mate."

Robin nodded thanks. "This year, for your meal, you must be accompanied by a cockney."

Diana suppressed a laugh. *Easy.*

"Defined as a person who was born within earshot of the Bow Bells," added Errol.

"Precisely," said Robin. "The location should be something not easily achievable or accessible. I invite you all to use your imagination. As judge, I will decide which entry is the most remarkable, and of course I will need a photograph for the album."

"I have a question too," said Diana. "The person who is fulfilling the role of cockney in this challenge is in addition to the helper, yes?"

"You are a cockney yourself?"

"Technically. I might not have the dialect but, like my mother, I was born a cockney."

Oxnard jumped in. "Diana, how would you like to come with me tomorrow?"

Errol raised a hand. "Diana's my assistant! Go get your own cockney."

Discussion on which celebrities and public personages might or might not be cockneys lasted through most of the main course. Errol launched into an atrocious cockney accent at one point. But to Diana's ears, it was no worse that Dick van Dyke's infamous performance in *Mary Poppins*.

As the plates were cleared, Zaf leaned towards Diana. "Is your mum fond of egg sandwiches?"

She smiled. "Want me to ask her on your behalf?"

Zaf exchanged a look with Kamran across the table then gave her a nod.

Kamran gestured to Zaf. "So tell me, young man, how you enjoyed your day. Was it what you expected?"

Diana saw alarm cross Zaf's face.

"Well..." he said. "I've never had a day like it. The jury's out on whether I enjoyed it, I think I might still be in shock."

This made Kamran roar with laughter. "Very good answer. You will need to get over today so that you're ready for tomorrow."

"A nice meal and a good night's sleep should do the trick," said Zaf, with a wave to their surroundings.

On cue, the waiting staff entered with the desserts. Dark chocolate mousses surrounded by delicate sweet fresh berries were placed before them.

"The rooms here are very comfortable," said Errol. "Anything you need will be provided if you just ask."

Oxnard muttered under his breath. "Anything you need."

Errol stared at him. "Sorry Oxnard? Do you have some sort of problem?"

"No. No. It's all very nice. But we know you, Errol. You squeeze every one of your suppliers until they squeal for mercy."

"I get the best price for everything."

"Do not go there," said Kamran to his two friends, his voice low and his smile dropping.

"I'm not going anywhere," said Oxnard.

Kamran gave him a warning look. "We are here to celebrate our friend, not kick over his ashes."

Diana listened, wondering what secrets these men shared. Were any of them related to the person she was sure she had seen fall from the *Silver Salmon* the previous day?

Errol turned to Oxnard. "I host you here," he said in a fierce voice.

Oxnard shook his head. "We could have stayed on my yacht—"

"I host you here," Errol repeated. "I feed you. Yet you repay me by suggesting the failures that led to Tristram's death are mine, my company's." He waved a meaty hand in Kamran's direction. "The building had a Dadashov-made security and safety system."

Kamran's mouth fell open. "We are not having this conversation!"

Zaf and Alexsei had stopped talking. Zaf was watching the men while Alexsei stared down at the table. Diana had a feeling he'd heard this conversation, or others like it, before.

"Of course," snapped Oxnard, "you would like to bury it. Suppress your feelings the Dadashov way."

Kamran met his gaze. "If you hadn't badgered him to meet the completion date just so you could move your precious pieces into secure storage." He narrowed his eyes. "Will those cold lifeless canvasses give you comfort, give you love, in your autumn years, *friend*?"

"Gentlemen!" Robin's voice cut through their snide comments.

The men shrank back in their chairs and looked at her. Robin reminded Diana of a schoolteacher reprimanding a group of children.

The blonde woman looked at each of the older men in turn before she spoke. "I would suggest that you remember yourselves, and remember where you are."

Diana knew what she meant: arguing in front of strangers like herself and Zaf.

Oxnard cleared his throat and looked at Errol. "Apologies, dear chap. Sincerest apologies. Didn't mean to offend you as host."

"We are friends," replied Errol. "We know each other intimately, good and bad. There's nothing to apologise for."

Kamran studied his two friends. "Do you know, I look forward to seeing you two each year more than anything else. Yourself as well, Robin."

There was a moment's silence as the three old friends regarded each other. Diana waited.

Then Errol laughed. Kamran and Oxnard were soon joining in.

Diana sensed Alexsei's body language untense. He exchanged an awkward smile with Zaf. She looked back at the men, still laughing.

She knew that kind of laughter. The laughter of those tied together, handcuffed together, by a shared history. The kind of laughter that might easily spill into tears.

The rest of the meal passed peacefully. The desserts were washed down with a selection of herbal teas from the spa's 'Asian tea library'. Diana sipped a jasmine tea and waited for this dysfunctional group to call an end to their evening.

Kamran was the first to excuse himself, claiming he needed to plan for the next day. Errol asked Robin and Oxnard to join him for a nightcap in the study.

"Of course," said Robin.

Oxnard shook his head. "I was hoping to speak to Diana here a little."

"You're not stealing my assistant," Errol warned him.

"Nothing of the sort," replied Oxnard. "I just had something I wanted to discuss. A matter of cockney lore."

Diana raised her eyebrows, wondering what nonsense he'd been told.

Errol turned to her. "You don't have to if you don't want to."

Diana really wanted her bed, but couldn't abandon years of habitual politeness. "I'd be delighted to talk with Mr Pike."

Errol gave her a look and left with Robin for the promised nightcap. Zaf and Alexsei took that as their cue to leave as well.

After a few moments, Diana and Oxnard were alone at the dining table, strewn with glasses and bunched-up napkins.

She waited.

CHAPTER TWENTY-SEVEN

OXNARD LEANED back in his chair. He downed the last of his herbal tea and regarded Diana.

"Of course I want to steal you," he said.

"As an assistant?"

"As my guest cockney for the day."

"But I'm Mr van Blerk's helper."

"There's nothing in the rules that expressly prohibits chopping and changing."

"And leaving your competitor in the lurch?"

"All part of the fun."

Was this cheating? Or just short of it?

"I think you have an odd idea of fun, Mr Pike," Diana said.

Oxnard's eyes twinkled. "Do you know what fun is, Mrs...?"

"Bakewell. *Miss* Bakewell. You think I don't know what fun is?"

"Fun," he replied, "is a luxury. Entirely. Imagine our caveman ancestors. They spent all of their days hunting and foraging and gathering firewood, just so they could eat and stay warm and make little caveman babies. None of it was fun. Life was horrible."

"Is that so?" Diana didn't bother to argue that the cave paintings might suggest otherwise. And the making of the little cavemen babies wasn't necessarily a chore for all involved.

"Medieval peasants toiled the field six days a week and worshipped on the seventh in churches they were forced to build. Barely a handful of holy days each year in which they could gorge on what food they had, dance their little jigs and drink their weak beer. Not much in the way of fun."

Diana suppressed a yawn. "I see."

Oxnard became more animated, leaning into his topic. "Fun and leisure are modern concepts. The masses got their Spanish sunshine holidays in the seventies and eighties. Now is the era of 'Netflix and chill'. People, ordinary common people, are only now beginning to grasp what fun might be." He moved his chair closer to hers. "But some of us, the successful, the lucky, we were given a head start. We've been having fun for centuries. We ate the produce of the field. We commissioned the great churches and the beautiful art to go in them. We knew fun long before you did."

Diana bristled at the *you*.

"You and your kind are experts in it, are you?"

Oxnard pulled back. "My kind? Well, yes. So, just as the native American chaps couldn't comprehend the ships and the guns of the Pilgrim Fathers, so the regular man – or woman – can't comprehend what true fun is."

"That's an interesting theory," Diana said.

"Not a theory. And if you agree to be my guest tomorrow, then you can learn more. And on top of that..." He leaned forward. "Tomorrow, we could have a little chat about what you saw or thought you saw happening on my yacht."

Diana felt her breath catch.

"Oh, I saw what I saw," she said. "There was a man. He crept onto your boat and was then ejected over the side and into the water."

Oxnard's eyes didn't leave her face. "We were on the London Eye, at a great height. It'd be hard to say what was really going on down there. Especially since no one else saw a thing."

She swallowed. "A shame, that. Because anyone looking that way would have seen the same as me."

Oxnard shook his head. "You are wrong. Any view, even of something as concrete as a work of art, is open to mistaken interpretations. You are familiar with *The Scream* by Edvard Munch?"

"I am."

"Who is screaming?"

Diana considered. "The person in the foreground. They have their hands to their face. Their mouth is wide."

"Ah," said Oxnard. "So the person in the foreground doesn't have their hands over their ears, distraught by the sound of a scream they are hearing? Interesting."

Diana pursed her lips. "Mr Pike. Clever tricks aside, I saw the man. I saw him fall."

"You did not!"

"I did. And I know his name."

"What?"

This time, Oxnard looked surprised. *Good*, thought Diana. *I've rattled you.* She always tried to find the good in her clients, but this time, it was proving difficult.

"He is a man called Vernon Monroth," she told him.

He pulled in a breath. "How could you possibly deduce that?"

"Old Philbin, the man at the memorabilia shop. He recognised him from a drawing I showed him. Vernon Monroth. A man with an art background, I believe. Do you know him?"

Oxnard's face flickered. He hesitated before replying. "I know of the man," he said, finally. "We don't move in the same circles."

"That's interesting to know."

"What drawing? What drawing did you show him?"

"It is a long enough story and it is getting late," she said, standing up. "I shall not be accompanying you as your egg sandwich lunch companion tomorrow. You'll have to find your own cockney elsewhere. It shouldn't be hard. There's thousands of us."

Oxnard stood to bring himself level with her. As he did so, he brushed against his napkin and something slid out from under it. It landed with a tap on the floor between them.

Diana glanced down. "You've dropped something."

She bent to pick it up. It was a simple box, with a button set into it. It looked like a remote car key, except its surface was entirely metal and it had no logo or maker's mark. She held it out to him.

Oxnard took it, turned it over and passed it back to her. "That's not mine."

"It was under your napkin."

He peered at it. "No. Not mine. Never seen it before."

Diana pressed the button. Nothing happened.

"Not mine," Oxnard repeated.

She shrugged and slipped the little device into her handbag.

"It's been interesting talking to you," she said. "An education. Good night, Mr Pike."

CHAPTER TWENTY-EIGHT

DIANA SPENT the night in a delightful room at the Serenity Haven. In contrast to the austere white spaces downstairs, the accommodation upstairs had taken its inspiration from sleeper berths on old-fashioned trains. There was a dark wood sleigh bed, plenty of built-in storage space and jewel-coloured velvet drapery. The bathroom was fitted out with checkerboard tiles, chrome plumbing and fluffy towels. It was like being on a cabin on the Orient Express, albeit one with its own coffee machine.

She rose early and set out for Baker Street tube. From there she took the Hammersmith and City line thirteen stops to Bromley-by-Bow. Here the Underground became an overground and she came up beside the dual carriageway that cut Bromley-by-Bow in two.

Commercialisation and construction had changed this part of London dramatically during Diana's lifetime. She passed high rises and crossed a supermarket car park before she reached the far more picturesque House Mill. A row of eighteenth-century buildings in light brown stone stood at the edge of the waterside. House Mill was a tidal mill, powered by water coming up and down the Thames. The two conical-shaped oast house kilns loomed over the other buildings.

Against the brutal modernity that had seized this corner of London, this place had an almost rustic charm.

Diana's mum's place was a flat just overlooking the Stanstead Mill Stream which flowed south into the Thames. Diana rapped on the door and rang the bell. She watched as her mum's white hair appeared through the frosted glass, then smiled as the door was opened.

Her mum looked her up and down. "Tea's just brewed."

Diana nodded. "Then I'm right on time."

Beverley Bakewell turned towards the kitchen. She waved a hand at the tea things and continued to the balcony over-looking the duckweed-covered stream out back.

"You want toast?" said Beverley. "You know where it is." She sat down at her little outdoor table.

Diana brought the tea things through.

Her mum had lived alone for the fifteen years since Diana's dad had died. She always seemed self-contained, content with her lot. Not that she wasn't sociable: the karaoke night at her local on Devas Street wasn't karaoke night unless Beverley got up to do some Bonnie Tyler. And Diana found Beverley's satis-faction and confidence in old age reassuring.

She'd spent the last two days watching Kamran and Alexsei Dadashov, considering how people eventually became like their parents. If her future was to become another Beverley Bakewell, then she could do worse.

Diana poured tea into two mugs.

"Did they find him?" asked her mum.

"Who?" said Diana.

"The man you saw fall in the Thames."

Diana had mentioned it to her on the phone.

"They did not," she said.

Beverley tutted and spooned four sugars into her tea. Diana had no idea how Beverley was so slim, skinny even, given her sugar intake.

"Your cousin Bertie had a mate who jumped in at Waterloo Bridge. Didn't come up again until the following Easter."

"Cousin Bertie?" Diana asked. "As in Freddie's son, Bertie?"

"No, that's Bertie Chappell. I'm talking about your aunt Reenie's nephew Bertie. Him and Sydney run the boats out of Rotherhithe."

"Bertie O'Shea?"

"That's the one."

Diana's family tree was a massive web of siblings, cousins and second cousins. Bertie O'Shea was either a second or third cousin, not much younger than her.

"And I remember," her mum continued, "he said that his mate would come up again at Greenwich." She slurped her tea. "He didn't reckon on it taking so long but he was right. That side of the family. No one knows the river better. Long line of Watermen and Lightermen, ain't they?"

The Company of Watermen and Lightermen were one of the hundred or more guilds and livery companies in London. Their history stretched back to the Middle Ages, a union for those who plied the waters of the Thames, delivering either passengers or goods.

The Guild of Tourism was the one Diana knew best. She'd earned her certification with them, and hoped that Zaf would soon follow suit. It had its ancient roots in the old Parish Constables' Guild.

"Maybe they'll know where my bloke will turn up," she said and sipped her tea.

She looked out over the water. It wasn't the most attractive of London waterways, but being near water still eased her mind.

She put her mug down and looked at her mum. "I'd like to take you out today."

"*Out* out?"

"*Out* out."

Beverley sniffed. "How d'you know I haven't got something on?"

Diana cocked her head. "Have you?"

"No. But I might've done. Where are you taking me out?"

"Well... it's more of a favour you could do me."

Beverley straightened in her chair and Diana suppressed a smile. Her mum always enjoyed being useful. Another family trait.

"What favour?" Beverley asked.

"You remember Zaf?"

Beverley licked her wrinkled lips in thought. "The young scallywag you've taken under your wing?"

"If you like. He and I are engaged in an... endeavour."

"A what?"

"A competition, I suppose. It's for work. He needs a cockney to help him."

"You're a cockney."

"I'm helping someone else. Basically, he wants to take you out for lunch. For an egg sandwich, to be precise."

"I like egg."

"I know you do."

"Today?"

"If you're alright with it, Mum, he'll probably collect you in the next hour or so. I don't know the details but I promise it'll be interesting."

There was a twinkle of amusement in Beverley's expression. "Well, this *is* intriguing. And I didn't think I had anything to look forward to except *Loose Women* and a game of cribbage down at the community centre."

CHAPTER TWENTY-NINE

Zaf was the first in the dining room for breakfast.

It took him a few minutes to convince the waiter that he just wanted a regular coffee and not something made from obscure South American beans or filtered through some process invented by mystical monks. Something like a regular coffee eventually appeared before him.

He sipped it and wondered if he had the courage to ask for just toast. Just white toast with some butter. He feared he might be offered unusual grains and yak's butter.

Alexsei entered. As he pushed the door open there was a shout in the corridor.

"Salvatore Ferragamo," a member of staff called to another. "She says she's not leaving without it."

The door swung closed and the voices abated. Alexsei scanned the room, then bent to give Zaf a peck on the cheek.

"I saw that," said Zaf.

"Saw what?"

"Are you embarrassed to be with me?"

Alexsei frowned. "No. Not at all. But you know that my father has..."

"Has other plans for the one true son and heir of his dynasty?"

Alexsei smiled. "Possibly. Possibly precisely that."

"But we *will* tell him?"

Alexsei nodded. "We will. And you found my father... tolerable yesterday?"

Zaf nodded. A waitress hovered near them. Time to ask for that toast, perhaps? "He knows his own mind," he said.

"Yes, he does." He gestured towards Zaf's coffee and the waitress hurried away. *Too late.*

"He's not the worst boss I have worked for," Zaf said. "Not by far."

"He is not your boss."

"For the next two days I'll think of him like that. How about Oxnard Pike?"

Alexsei sighed. "Definitely treats me like he is my boss."

The door opened and Diana entered, her cheeks flushed.

"My mum says yes," she said, pulling out a chair.

"She'll join me and Mr Dadashov?" asked Zaf.

Diana nodded. "She regards you as something of a scallywag."

"Is that good, or bad?"

A shrug. "I think it's meant with affection."

Diana ordered Eggs Benedict and a large pot of tea. Zaf took the opportunity to finally request toast. He was told it would be on sourdough bread, which wasn't too far away from what he had been thinking of.

As they waited for the food, Errol, Oxnard, Kamran and Robin joined them. Oxnard had brought a newspaper. Zaf watched him grappling with it. Who still bought printed newspapers?

"I have no further instructions for today's challenge," said Robin, a cup of coffee in one hand. "But I do have the body-cams for everyone to put on before they leave—"

Errol had raised a hand.

Robin frowned then nodded her head. "Yes. A change to the line-up today."

Errol looked at Oxnard. "I assume you have poached Diana from me."

"Not at all," said Oxnard, rustling his paper. "Wouldn't dream of it."

Errol's cheek twitched, then he straightened in his chair. "So. In order to be prepared for all eventualities, I have engaged the services of a new helper."

"What?" asked Kamran. "You can only have one assistant. And she is already here."

"But I'm allowed to switch if I like," Errol replied.

Diana looked surprised. "You're getting rid of me?"

Errol eyed her. "Just following your suggestion."

"*My* suggestion?"

"She'll be here any minute." Errol met Diana's gaze. "Diana, I thank you for your assistance yesterday. Truly. If there hadn't been some mucking about with the rules, we'd have won. But, it's like you said, you can't embrace the fun. You're too hidebound by your... your principles. I need someone a bit more calculating, someone with bite."

"I didn't say any of that."

The South African frowned. "Didn't you? That's what I heard."

There was a quiet knock at the dining room door and a woman entered.

"You're replacing me with Ariadne Webb?" Diana said. Her face had paled and one fist was clenched on the table.

Zaf chewed his bottom lip. He knew how Diana felt about Ariadne.

"Good morning, everyone," said Ariadne.

Errol leaned back, beaming. "ACE Tours were good enough to release her to me for the rest of the week."

Diana had described Ariadne to Zaf. She hadn't used the word *nemesis*, but that sounded pretty close to what she was.

"I like this woman," said Errol. "She seems highly competent and perhaps not so... prone to quibbling over instructions."

Diana's knuckles were growing white, but her face was calm.

"Very well, Mr van Blerk," she said. "The choice is yours to make, of course."

She looked at Oxnard. Zaf hoped he was in need of a cockney, for Diana's sake.

"No," said Oxnard. "I have my new cockney lunch date already lined up." He placed his napkin on the table. "I do not require your services. Not today."

"I see," said Diana, her voice terse.

Ariadne threw a smile at Diana. "Diana. It's always a delight to see you, however briefly. It seems you are surplus to requirements."

"So it seems," said Diana, standing. "Have a good day everybody. Enjoy the challenge."

Zaf couldn't stomach this. He stood and followed her.

In the corridor leading to reception, he caught up with her. She was hurrying along, muttering.

"He can't do that," Zaf said.

Diana turned. Her phone was in her hand, buzzing. She

ignored it. "I very much think Errol van Blerk can do exactly as he pleases."

Zaf approached her. "But to sack you, right in front of everyone!"

"I've not been sacked."

"But you were the only one who worked out the location of the house on the postcard! Is he mad?"

"It doesn't matter if he's mad, Zaf. He's rich."

Zaf scowled, his mind churning. "Such selfishness."

"Stock in trade for these men, it seems. I should feel sorry you're still saddled with them."

Zaf glanced back towards the dining room. "Kamran's not so bad, if you don't count Alexsei being weird about telling him we're an item."

Diana's mouth was pressed into a tight line. "Those men. They've got some secrets, haven't they?"

"How so?"

"I told Oxnard about the man on the boat, Vernon Monroth."

"And?"

"He knew him," she said. "He said he knew *of* him, but he hesitated, it gave him away. He knew the man." She sniffed. "I've got family who work on the Thames. I might get their opinion of where the body might have washed up."

Zaf nodded. If Diana said she'd seen this man fall into the river, then he believed her.

She put a hand on his arm. "There's something... dark going on here."

He couldn't help but smile. "Sticking your nose in?"

She narrowed her eyes, a smile playing at her lips. "Diana Bakewell, one of the invisible and ignored women. Rejected by these self-centred billionaires. Yes, I'm sticking my nose in."

She looked at her phone and pressed a button.

"Voicemail," she said, putting it to her ear. Her eyes widened as she listened.

"It's Kensington Police Station," she said. "They want me to come in and talk to them."

Zaf felt his heart rate pick up. "Might be news about our man."

She flashed him a look. "Only one way to find out."

CHAPTER THIRTY

Zaf wondered how he'd fit into the world of billionaires when they could treat Diana like a disposable asset. How could he be sure that Kamran wouldn't do the same thing? Or even Alexsei? And how would Kamran's attitude change once he knew the truth about Zaf and his son?

He pushed down his worries as he joined Kamran in a limo bound for Bromley-by-Bow. Zaf was glad not to be driving again.

"Diana's mum has agreed to come with us," he told Kamran. There was a message from Diana with her mum's address. "She's in her eighties so she can't go up ladders, in case you're thinking of eating your sandwich on top of one of the columns in Trafalgar Square."

Kamran laughed. "I think Oxnard did that back near the beginning. We need to be more creative these days. What is the name of Diana's mum?"

"Beverley."

"I cannot wait to meet her. But we will be careful with a

woman of such an age. If there are ladders, then you will carry her, yes?"

Zaf eyed Kamran. Was he joking?

Beverley Bakewell was waiting when they arrived, her face made up and wearing a pink silk blouse. She opened the door of her flat and looked them up and down.

"You're Zaf," she said to him.

"I am."

She glanced at Kamran. "Door to door double-glazing salesman?"

"Not quite, madam. Not quite." Kamran took her hand in a gentle but warm grip.

Beverley looked as if someone had let the air out of a Diana-shaped balloon. They had similar features, but Beverley was shorter and a bit puckered. Zaf would never tell either woman that, though.

"Come in, come in!" she said. "I've got the eggs on the boil."

Zaf glanced at Kamran. "Beverley, that's kind of you. But I'm sure Kamran wasn't expecting you to make the sandwiches."

She waved a hand, heading to the kitchen. "I like an egg sandwich as much as the next person, but I don't care for those supermarket ones. Sloppy and flavourless. You know that the secret's to stir a teaspoon of vinegar in with the mayo, don't you?"

"I didn't know," said Zaf. "Did you, Kamran?"

"No I did not. Very pleased to meet you, Beverley, and I can't wait to try out your egg sandwich. I will cancel the picnic from The Ritz."

"Oh, he's a proper card, this one," Beverley said to Zaf.

"Definitely a salesman of some sort. You sit in the sitting room while I finish up."

The lounge of the little flat was old-fashioned but comfortable. Kamran, his movements stiff, walked over to a teak display unit and picked up a picture that showed a much younger Diana grinning at the camera.

"This is in a television studio I think?" he said.

Zaf looked at the photo. He'd seen it before but not recognised the setting. "It is, you're right."

He imagined it had been taken when Diana was riding success with the hit single *Count Me In*. He stared at the picture, but there wasn't much to see beside Diana smiling at the camera.

Zaf sat on the velour sofa and Kamran took the single chair.

"Diana is a woman who knows her own mind," said Kamran. Zaf wondered if Alexsei's father had been reading his thoughts.

"She is," said Zaf. "I wouldn't mind being like her when I'm older."

Kamran nodded. "She is a good mentor, I think. You are lucky. I suspect that she may have challenged Errol's authority, which has led to him replacing her. I feel certain that he will regret this."

Zaf was reluctant to be drawn into talk of the men's rivalries. "I don't know," he said. "Ariadne will do a good job, I'm sure."

"Good. A diplomatic answer."

Beverley bustled in with a tray of tea and put it onto the low table. "I'll just be a few minutes. Pour me one with milk and four sugars when it's sat for a minute, will you, Zaf, love?"

"Will do, Beverley."

She gave him a look. "It's Bev. Don't be so formal."

"Thanks, Bev."

"That's more like it."

"So," Zaf said to Kamran as she left the room, "I guess this challenge is one you can prepare for ahead of time?"

"That is true," replied Kamran. "We think about it and make arrangements, of course we do. When Mrs Bakewell comes in and sits down I will tell you what it is that I propose to do."

Zaf poured the tea, itching to know the plan.

"It is interesting that we were all able to get our cockney guests with no difficulty," said Kamran. "Maybe my Alexsei knows such people."

"He knows people from all over town," said Zaf.

"Alexsei and you are good friends?"

Zaf swallowed. "We... er..." He gave a nervous laugh. "For a long time, I thought he hated me. He can be... fierce."

Kamran was about to speak when Beverley came into the room.

"Oh tea, thanks!" she said and sat down next to Zaf. "What is it we're doing today, then?"

Zaf watched Kamran as he preened proudly at his audience of two.

"Bev," began Kamran.

The old woman looked up from her cup. "Beverley. I don't know you."

Zaf suppressed a grin.

"Beverley," said Kamran. "I do apologise. We are going to eat our egg sandwiches in the most unusual of places."

"Where?" she asked.

"Today, we will be eating our egg sandwiches at the bottom of the river Thames."

Kamran looked between Bev and Zaf, his expression smug.

Bev hooted out a laugh. Zaf frowned.

"I beg your pardon?" he whispered.

CHAPTER THIRTY-ONE

DIANA CONSIDERED herself knowledgeable about London, but that didn't mean she'd been down every street. Kensington Police Station, housed in a sturdy but unremarkable red-brick building on Earls Court Road, was new to her.

She introduced herself to the officer on the reception desk and a few minutes later a sergeant came through to meet her. The slim Asian woman shook Diana's hand.

"I'm Sergeant Sarah Khan. Very glad you could come in. We have a man in our cells we're keen to get rid of and I hope you can put everything in order."

Diana was surprised. "In the cells? I thought he was dead."

"Dead? We picked him up, very much alive."

"Vernon Monroth?"

The sergeant gave her a quizzical look. "A Mr Newton Crombie."

"Sorry? Newton is in the cells?"

The sergeant looked puzzled. "Is there a dead person we should be aware of?"

"You're aware of him, I mean the police are. I'm not sure if any of you believe me though."

The sergeant raised an eyebrow. "Fascinating. Let's get you signed in."

Sergeant Khan gave Diana a visitor badge and led her to an interview room. As they reached the door, a large figure approached.

"Ah. I thought I had missed you."

Diana knew Detective Chief Inspector Clint Sugarbrook. She'd spent a few days in his company when he'd interviewed all of her tour party over the unexplained death of a man on top of an open deck bus. Diana had provided him with as much assistance as possible but still felt he saw her as an interfering busybody.

"Detective Chief Inspector," said Diana. "Were you the one who arrested Newton?"

He frowned. "Nothing to do with me. I just heard that my... acquaintance Diana Bakewell was in the building so I asked Sergeant Khan here if I could sit in."

The interview room was small and Clint Sugarbrook, the son of a professional boxer, was a very large man. It was a squeeze.

"Is Newton alright?" asked Diana as she sat down.

Sergeant Khan took out her notebook. "I'm hoping this is all a misunderstanding. We arrested Mr Crombie late last night in Harrods."

Diana stared. "Harrods? The high-end department store?"

"On a charge of shoplifting."

Diana ran through the events of the last few days in her mind.

"It wasn't shoes, was it?" she asked.

Sergeant Khan nodded slowly. "So, you know about his habit?"

"It's not a habit. He doesn't normally go to Harrods. You've seen how he dresses."

An uncharitable person might have described Newton as a man who looked like he'd been dressed by his mum. Or possibly, as a man dressed as a post-war office clerk. He wore neat shirts and dull jumpers. The most exciting thing he owned was a knitted tank top.

"Where does he normally go?" asked Sergeant Khan. "For shoes?"

Diana frowned. "He was carrying a bag of shoes, I'm guessing. And he was arrested because, ah, because, er, a man walking round with a carrier bag of single women's shoes would look like he had a, er, *thing* for shoes."

"There are many varied and interesting people in this world," said Sergeant Khan. "Trust me. Most of them have come through here."

Diana shook her head. "Can I tell you what's really happening?" she asked.

"I'd love to hear that."

"It's a bit... unbelievable."

"I'm all ears," said the young sergeant.

"It's our cat, Gus. He lives in our bus depot on Chiltern Street. He's been going out and coming back with shoes, specifically women's shoes."

"Where does he find them?"

"We've no idea. Really we don't. Newton gathered them all together and I'm guessing he was doing a bit of... reverse shoplifting."

"So, you think the cat stole the shoes from Harrods?"

"No," said Diana. "I should imagine Newton's thought

processes were simpler. I think he was caught putting the shoes back in a place where they *might* belong."

Sergeant Khan dropped her notepad on the table and sat back.

"Astonishing."

"I know it sounds a little far-fetched," said Diana.

"It's astonishing that you've pretty much matched Newton Crombie's personal account. And, even more astonishing, I think I believe it."

"It's an unlikely turn of events," said DCI Sugarbrook.

"We have a very contrite Mr Crombie in our cells," said Sergeant Khan. "I think he'd be relieved and we'd be happy if we released him to your care. I shall inform Harrods that what we have here is a peculiar set of events caused by...."

"A moment of madness?" suggested Sugarbrook.

"And a grey tabby cat," added Diana.

Sergeant Khan put a hand on her notebook, then leaned across the table towards Diana. "Before we came in, you were talking about a dead man, Miss Bakewell?"

"Vernon Monroth," Diana confirmed. "I saw him fall in the Thames on Tuesday."

"And you called the police?"

"They searched the area. He never came up again. I assumed he had drowned."

"Are you going to get a reputation for being around when people die in unusual circumstances?" said Sugarbrook.

Diana eyed him. It had been her and Zaf who had found the body on the open-top bus.

"At least you're willing to accept that I saw him," she said. "Apparently, there were no other witnesses."

"It's hard to imagine that events can happen unnoticed in a city like London," said Sugarbrook. "But they do."

"Well, maybe you can have a word with the people in charge and get them to look again."

Sugarbrook regarded her for a moment then turned to Sergeant Khan. "Sergeant," he said, "do you want to process Newton Crombie's release? I'll walk Diana back out."

CHAPTER THIRTY-TWO

Diana was alone with Sugarbrook. The DCI looked at her across the table.

"What's this Vernon individual to you?" he asked.

"Nothing at all," she said. "I bumped into him once. Literally. He knows some men we've got as clients this week."

"I've got a friend on the Marine Policing Unit," said Sugarbrook. "Kenny. Solid bloke. I'll put a word in his ear. And this chap. Vernon...?"

"Monroth."

"Right. I'll see if he's been reported missing."

"Thank you."

"It's my job, Miss Bakewell. Nothing more. I'll take you to your colleague now."

The reception area was empty.

"I'll ask about your guy," said Sugarbrook, "but try to remember, Miss Bakewell, that just because something happens in London, doesn't mean it's any of your business."

She gave him a look. "Are you warning me off, Detective Chief Inspector?"

He smiled. "And what good would that do me? You wouldn't listen anyway."

A door opened and Newton Crombie, looking bleary-eyed and dishevelled, emerged in the company of Sergeant Khan.

"Oh, Diana," he said. "You can't imagine what I've been through."

"Nor do I want to," she said and reached out to straighten his shirt collar.

Sergeant Khan held out a carrier bag holding at least half a dozen women's shoes.

"They're not mine," said Newton.

"They don't belong to Harrods," said Sergeant Khan, "and they definitely don't belong to us, so I don't want to see them or you again."

Newton took them without meeting her eye.

Back at the Chartwell and Crouch depot, Diana went to put the kettle on.

"Tea, toast and then home to your family, I suggest," she said.

She turned to see Newton at the kitchen table, a laptop open in front of him.

"Tea, toast and home?" she repeated.

He shook his head. "It's time for Plan B."

Heaven help us.

"Yes?"

He took out one of the shoes. "I will list each of these on a selling site. If you help me with photos and descriptions, we can have them done in no time."

Diana looked at him. "Newton. It's not that I don't want to

help you, I really do. But I question the wisdom of this. Who will be searching for a single shoe?"

"Great point!" Newton smiled. "Let's create a list of keywords. What might you search for if you wanted only one shoe? Pirate cosplay? Unusual drinking vessel? Oddkins Bodkins?"

"Oddkins Bodkins?"

"It was a kids' TV show," he said. "The main character wore odd shoes and spoke with a funny accent. You must remember it?"

Diana shook her head. "Never heard of it. I'm really not sure anyone's going to be searching for that, Newton."

"You never know until you try. Photos please."

Reluctantly, Diana took pictures of the shoes. She sent them to Newton as he created listings that included fanciful keywords and careful descriptions.

"We're not doing all of them, are we?" she asked, half an hour later. "We could just do some and then see what happens."

Newton pursed his lips. "You're right. Experimentation is key. We'll do the rest in batches. Aren't you meant to be escorting rich fellows around London today?"

Diana grunted. "My services aren't required."

"Oh, that's good. Day to yourself."

She sighed. "I think I might call in on my cousin, Bertie."

"Is that so?" Newton peered at the laptop screen.

Diana nodded. "I need to ask a few questions about the Thames..."

CHAPTER THIRTY-THREE

Z AF SAT between Bev and Kamran in the limo taking them to
the river. He had a thousand and one questions for Kamran,
mostly about how the multimillionaire intended to have lunch
at the bottom of the Thames.

"D'you know what a dangerous environment the Thames
can be?" Bev said. "Tidal drop of seven metres."

"I understand," replied Kamran, unbothered.

"Those currents are wicked too, up to four knots. My family's been on the river for generations and none of us'd be daft
enough to get in there." She jabbed him on the shoulder.
"You've got to respect the water."

Kamran turned to her. "I can assure you that there will be
no danger, Beverley."

Diana's mum made a clicking sound with her teeth. "You
can never go on the river thinking that. Didn't you *hear* what I
said about respect?"

"Very well. All of the risks have been considered carefully
and fully mitigated."

"Kamran," said Zaf. "How exactly are we going to do this?

I've never tried diving, but I can't see how you'd eat an egg sandwich wearing breathing apparatus."

Kamran tapped his nose. "Ah, but we will not be diving in the sense that you describe. We will be inside a submersible."

"Like a submarine?"

"That is correct."

Zaf shared a glance with Bev. Part of him was willing her to flatly refuse to do such a ridiculous thing, but instead she looked intrigued.

"Show me," she said.

"A picture?" Kamran pulled out his phone and searched. He held it up.

Zaf and Bev leaned in to look. It was a transparent sphere mounted in an armchair-shaped craft. Zaf could see chairs mounted inside the sphere. They looked like bucket seats from a fancy sports car.

"Oh my word," said Beverley.

"Wow," said Zaf.

"I can't wait!" declared the old woman.

"That's the spirit." Kamran gave her a wink.

Zaf wasn't quite as keen, but he swallowed down his nervousness and smiled with as much enthusiasm as he could muster.

"We're going in a submarine," he whispered.

CHAPTER THIRTY-FOUR

DIANA HEADED OVER TO ROTHERHITHE. She'd not seen Bertie and Sydney O'Shea since a distant niece's wedding some years back, but the moment she'd got hold of Bertie on the phone, he'd invited her to come and visit. The O'Sheas were a pair of Bermondsey boys but ran boats out of South Dock in nearby Rotherhithe.

Like much of the East End, the traditional buildings and old industry had been swept away by redevelopment and modernisation. Diana wasn't a nostalgic fool and knew that much of what had been replaced were slums and abandoned warehouses. But still, she was happiest when she saw those glimpses of traditional London and the old ways of life. There were plenty of old-style Dutch barges moored up and even a few sailing ships, not just the playthings of the rich but actual sailing ships that would once have been used to deliver cargo up and down the river.

Bertie waved at her from his boat. The hull was long and low with a high wheelhouse up near the bow. It looked like a beefed-up version of the boat from *Jaws*. Any monster of the deep would have a hard time sinking this chunky vessel.

"Permission to come aboard?" she called from the pier.

Bertie waved her on. "Come here, you daft gal."

However you measured him, Bertie was a big bloke. He resembled a strategically shaved bear, a grizzly, grey bear these days. He enveloped Diana in a hug then gripped her arms as though testing them for strength.

He grinned. "You look well, don't ya?"

"It's been a while." She looked past him. "Sydney with you today?"

"Nah, on me tod today. Sydney said the wrong thing to a bloke down the pub, and e's a bit of a two-and-eight today. You gonna crew for me, right?"

She hesitated. "Right."

Five minutes later the boat, the *Polychrest*, was chugging away into the body of the Thames. Diana looked out of the wheelhouse at the water, steely blue and estuary brown in places. Deep, ancient and uncontrollable. She shuddered.

The boat cut a swathe through the water but even so they rocked from side to side, the high wheelhouse like the tip of a slow metronome.

"You got much work on at the moment?" she asked Bertie.

"Plenty. Port of London's always on our case. Act like they own the bloody river. Don't realise we were here first. Good job you caught me today, though. I'm hauling containers from tomorrow all the way through to next weekend."

"So nothing today?"

He gave her a sideways look. "Taking my favourite cousin out. Knock some of that North London softness out of you."

She smiled. "Favourite cousin, huh?"

"Tied first place. Still favourite." They were chugging

down the Thames, going with the flow of the tide. "You gonna tell me about this body, then?"

Diana recounted Vernon Monroth's fall into the Thames. She had replayed it so many times in her mind, she didn't know what was real, and what was her imagination filling in the gaps.

"And what time was that?" he asked, pulling rolled-up and well-thumbed maps from a storage cubby.

Diana checked her phone for the time of her call to the emergency services. "Eleven fifteen am."

Bertie laid out a map of the Thames and weighed down the ends of it. There were lines all along the Thames. Tides? Depths? She wasn't sure.

"Here," he said, pointing at the stretch of the river running past the London Eye. "Anything that goes in there can get snagged under Hungerford Bridge or Waterloo Bridge, but the river would have been heading out at quite a lick at that time." He traced a line along the curve of the great river, past the City of London, Wapping and onward to Greenwich, Woolwich and beyond.

"Where do you think he ended up?" she asked.

Bertie chuckled. "Your old mum told you that story of how I predicted where Mickey Savage's body turned up? Pure luck. You can't second guess the river. Could be anywhere."

Diana tried not to show her disappointment. "We're not going to find him then?"

He chuckled. "Sure, and then we're going to pick the winning lottery numbers. So who is this guy to you?"

"Nothing," she said. "Just a man no one else saw die."

Bertie nodded solemnly. "You know how many people die in the Thames each year? Dozens. Jumpers, fallers. Then there's the ones who've been killed then dumped. The marine police are fishing them out every week."

"Sounds unpleasant."

"There are worse ways to go." He stuck out his bottom lip. "Not many, though."

They were passing the Isle of Dogs on their left. Up ahead was the spikey dome of the O2 Arena. Somewhere below them, the Blackwall tunnels carried four lanes of traffic under the Thames.

"Vernon Monroth lived on the Thames," said Diana. "He had a houseboat."

"What kind?"

She shook her head. "He had it up at Chelsea but had to move it. The *Fighting Temeraire*. That was the name."

Bertie looked at her. "Like the Turner painting." He caught her look of surprise. "Yes, I know my art, Diana. The *Fighting Temeraire* is a painting of a ship being towed away to be scrapped, ain't it?"

She nodded. "Hardly an auspicious name for a boat of any kind."

"Yeah, I thought that when..." Bertie clicked his fingers in recollection. "Bloody hell, I know where it is. Wanna do a drive by?"

"You do? I mean, yes. Why not?"

"Give us something to aim for while I fill you in on a little knowledge of the Thames."

The *Polychrest* accelerated. The engine chugged harder and the wake of the boat grew foamier.

CHAPTER THIRTY-FIVE

THE LIMO DROPPED ZAF, Kamran and Mrs Bakewell at St Katherine's Dock, near Tower Bridge.

"Are you nervous about this, Zaf?" Kamran asked, offering a hand to help Beverley out of the car.

Was this another test? Zaf felt like everything had been, since this whole thing had started, but that was probably just his anxiety about his relationship with Alexsei and how Kamran would react.

He searched for the right words. "Maybe a bit of nervous anticipation. Excitement."

"A reasonable human reaction," said Kamran. "Beverley, your robust attitude to risk is noted and I would like to assure you that I have an operations team who will address any concerns. We are about to meet them now."

Kamran led them along a walkway. St Katherine's Dock was home to many fine boats, the restaurants and drinking establishments reminding Zaf of how much wealthier these people were.

"Here we are," said Kamran. "Step aboard, if you will."

It was a small boat. Zaf wondered if he'd be right to call it a rubber dinghy.

"This is a RIB," said Kamran, as if he'd read Zaf's mind. "A reinforced inflatable boat."

Zaf liked the sound of the 'reinforced' part, but 'inflatable' reminded him of those coastguard warnings about getting out of your depth on a Lilo.

They stepped onto the boat, Beverley's footing much more secure than Zaf's. A pair of silent employees released the ropes and manoeuvred it onto the open Thames.

Zaf realised that they were going to be transferred from the small boat onto a larger one. They pulled up alongside a low flat barge moored alongside a pier in the middle of the river. Towards the aft was a winch, and attached to it the submersible Kamran had shown them.

Only now did he start to believe the bit about the submarine.

"Is that how we get into the water?" The idea of being dangled from a crane didn't appeal.

Kamran led them towards the submersible where a lean man in black was making checks, ticking items off on a clipboard.

"Faisal is chief of operations," said Kamran.

"Pleased to meet you." Faisal shook their hands and waggled the clipboard. "Last minute inspections." He pulled a sheet from his clipboard. "Here's a copy for each of you to keep. I think you'll find everything is in order."

Bev took the document, glanced at it, then peered into the submersible. "It's bigger than I imagined."

"Aye," said Faisal, "but we'll have plenty of room on the course we'll take. The tide is high and we won't get in the path of any larger vessels."

Zaf gave a light tap on the sphere. "Is this glass or plastic?" He wasn't sure which answer would make him less unhappy.

"It's an acrylic pressure hull," replied Faisal. "All-round visibility is a priority for these vessels. They're used for film-making as well as leisure. Part of our prep is to make sure it's totally clean. Give passengers the best possible experience."

Leisure? Zaf wasn't so sure. He pulled his fingers away, worried he'd left marks.

"Have you taken this thing down into the Thames before?" asked Bev.

Faisal nodded. "We arrived here yesterday and did a test dive. It went smoothly, although the view isn't what you might get in clearer waters."

Zaf felt that he was in safe hands. Faisal's quiet competence was reassuring.

Was he even beginning to look forward to it?

———

Thank you for reading *Death on the Thames*, the story continues in *Death at St Paul's*. It is available on Amazon.

CHAPTER THIRTY-SIX

BERTIE'S CLAIM TO know the location of Vernon Monroth's houseboat turned out to be optimistic. The *Polychrest* chugged westward, pausing near various marinas and mooring points while he looked. Soon they were passing through the Thames Flood Barrier.

"We go much beyond Woolwich and we'll be into Rainham Marshes and the countryside," said Bertie.

Now they were leaving London proper, Diana's knowledge started to get fuzzy. She took a deep breath, determined to enjoy herself and not just think about the poor man who'd fallen in the river.

"Gallions Point!" cried Bertie.

He spun the wheel and turned left through a narrow cutting. Ahead was a wide marina with the runways of London City Airport at one side.

"He had to move right out here," said Bertie and pointed.

Sure enough, moored along the concrete wall were a number of vessels including a square-ended houseboat with the name *Fighting Temeraire* painted on its side in peeling letters.

"You certain the geezer's dead?" asked Bertie.

"Why?" said Diana.

"Well, you could take a look on board. I'll draw alongside."

The *Polychrest* slowed to a crawl and Diana stepped out onto the deck at the point closest to the houseboat. There was the continuous barking of a dog from somewhere, a terrier yip.

"Is it trespassing if I go on board without permission?" she shouted to Bertie.

"Depends if you get caught!"

Diana judged her moment and stepped over. She grabbed a railing. The houseboat rocked in the swell created by the *Polychrest*.

She'd always had romantic notions of houseboats, which the *Fighting Temeraire* utterly failed to live up to. Vernon Monroth's houseboat had square sides and boxy windows that made it feel like someone had plonked a conservatory or a potting shed on a simple hull and launched it into the Thames. The wood and the metal-framed windows gave it a dated and temporary feel. It reminded Diana of the pre-fab houses people had lived in after the Blitz.

She worked her way around the outside. She cupped her hands against a condensation-streaked window and peered in. The interior was gloomy.

A wiry apparition appeared at the window, causing her to start. A terrier planted its front feet on the back of a sofa and barked at her, repeatedly.

She composed herself. *It's just a dog.*

"OK," she said in a soothing voice. "Didn't mean to surprise you."

The dog gave a final bark, licked its nose and tilted its head at her.

"Is your owner in?" she asked.

The dog tilted its head the other way.

"Have you been in there since Tuesday?" Diana asked.

The dog turned and jumped down from the sofa.

Diana felt sorry for the dog, cooped up for so long. And she knew she should be wary. But she also knew that this gave her an excuse to go inside.

She worked her way round to a splintered and rotten wooden door, held secure with a padlock on a brass bracket. In her purse, she had a manicure set and a pair of nail clippers with an edge that worked as an impromptu screwdriver. It took less than a minute to remove two brass screws and open the door with the padlock still attached.

A wiry blurry of lightning shot out, passed her legs, leapt the metre gap between houseboat and dock and pelted off down the dockside.

"Hey!" she shouted.

But the high-speed terrier was gone.

"He'll probably be back," Diana told herself and went inside without stopping to remember that she no longer had a reason to.

In contrast to the decrepit exterior, the houseboat's interior was cosy. There was a large living room and smaller spaces beyond. Bamboo furniture crowded the living room with over-stuffed bookcases behind. A Turkish coffee set sat on a table in the centre of the room, beside some heavy art books. Creepers hung from macramé pot holders, a giant cheese plant loomed in one corner and the air smelled of vegetative decay and the ghosts of meals cooked in the past.

"Hello, Vernon," she said to no one.

She moved through the space, thinking of the man she knew was dead.

On a desk in a corner was a mountain of papers, a pair of

lever arch files and a laptop that quite possibly belonged in a museum.

Diana opened a lever arch file. In a plastic wallet was a colour photocopy of an oil painting and behind it a series of scrawled notes. She was about to take the sheets out when she saw something on the desk tucked under the folder. It was the edge of a postcard.

She held her breath. She knew that art nouveau design.

She pulled out the postcard. It was one of the whimsical fairy designs.

"Schmucker," she muttered, remembering the artist's name.

She turned it over.

It was addressed to Vernon Monroth, at the *Fighting Temeraire*. The simple message was chilling.

We will discuss your demands. 11am *next Tuesday. The* Silver Salmon. *Moored at London County Hall.*

It was unsigned.

"Oh, my," Diana whispered.

Vernon had had a number of these cards on him when she'd bumped into him outside the London Eye. Had they all borne messages from the same sender?

With a growing sense of unease, she pushed the folder aside and searched the desk in case there were any more.

"Just what the hell do you think you're doing?" came a voice from behind her.

Diana gripped the card, and turned.

CHAPTER THIRTY-SEVEN

Zaf's initial *Hunt for Red October* vision wasn't as far from the mark as he'd imagined. The submersible was lowered into the water without passengers on board, and then they were transferred from the inflatable boat into a hole in the top. The process felt more precarious than Zaf would have liked.

He closed his eyes as Faisal guided him in through the hole after Bev, Kamran coming in after them and Faisal bringing up the rear and closing the hatch. They wore lifejackets that Faisal said would inflate automatically in case of emergency. In an uninflated state, it was like wearing a chunky harness.

Bev clutched the coolbox containing the sandwiches. She'd resisted all Zaf's offers to take them from her, insisting that it was her job to make sure they remained intact for their underwater picnic.

Underwater picnic. The thought sent a shiver through him.

Bev was Diana's mum; she had to be ancient. So how was she so cool about all this? Made from the same steely stuff as her daughter, no doubt.

"Are we all ready?" Faisal asked, to nods and grunts. There was a soft electric whirring as they started to descend.

Electricity and water, Zaf thought as they went down. *Never a good combination.*

It was both alarming and exciting to see the water swirling up the outside of the sphere. Zaf watched the childlike wonder on Kamran and Bev faces.

"Look at that!" said Bev. "We always had a saying when I was a kid that if the tea hadn't brewed long enough in the pot then it was like it'd had a quick dip in the Thames. Takes me right back."

Zaf and Kamran laughed. The water definitely had a sepia tint, which got darker as they sank further. There were lights on the submersible, so they could see for a few feet in every direction, including below their feet.

"You'll see the bottom just below," said Faisal. "We're not deep at all. Now we will take a small circular trip, but you'll appreciate that we must confine our activities to a restricted area which we've agreed with the Port of London Authority."

"Aye aye, Captain!" said Kamran with an extravagant salute.

CHAPTER THIRTY-EIGHT

Diana turned to see two figures looming in the doorway of Vernon Monroth's houseboat.

The younger one was slender with a shaved head and a nose that looked like it had been broken more than once. The older one had grey temples and a glowering presence that filled all the available space. They looked like the kind of men most people wouldn't want to meet down a back alley in the East End.

But Diana knew them.

"Ernie!" she cried in relief.

Big Ernie Holland's expression changed as soon as he recognised her.

"Diana? What on earth are you doing 'ere, darling?"

Big Ernie was a man Diana referred to as an uncle, despite definitely not being an uncle at all. He'd been a friend of Diana's parents and she'd known him all her life. He was someone she was relieved to be friends with, mainly because she was sure it was preferable to *not* being friends with him. The younger man was Chaz Chase, sometime barman, sometime cabby and full-time dodgy and dangerous type.

Diana ignored Ernie's question. "What are *you* doing here?" she replied.

"Dropping in on an old friend." Ernie beamed at her in a way that suggested Vernon Monroth might not have been pleased at a visit from an 'old friend' like Ernie.

"This is Vernon Monroth's place," she said.

"That's right. Slippery fish of a man keeps moving it. I heard he recently shuffled off his mortal coil."

"How did you hear that?"

"Friend of a friend on the force. Rumours that he took a dive into the Thames and didn't bother coming back up."

She nodded. "I saw it."

"Blimey," said Chaz.

Ernie sniffed. "So, with nothing but respect for the dear departed in our hearts, we thought we'd pop down and collect some items of sentimental value."

Diana stared at him. "You've come to rob him?"

Ernie clutched his heart as if mortally wounded.

"We don't rob, Diana. You have mistaken us for thieving crooks. I am merely collecting what is owed to me."

"Vernon Monroth was in debt to you?"

"And to others besides."

Chaz began poking around shelves, turning over items, setting aside anything that seemed of potential value.

Ernie tilted his head in the general direction of Bertie's boat outside. "I see you've brought young Bertie O'Shea with you. What are you doing here?"

"I told you. I saw him die."

"Hardly a reason to be breaking and entering, my love."

He was right. She took a breath.

"I saw him die and no one else did. As far as the rest of the world is concerned, he's just vanished." She waggled the post-card. "The day he died, he was on a yacht belonging to this man, Oxnard Pike. The *Silver Salmon*. Monroth was some sort of art dealer, possibly not the most honest of them."

Ernie laughed and Chaz threw in a light chuckle.

"A deep understatement there," said Ernie. "You want to know about Vernon Monroth?"

"I do," Diana replied. "Everything you know."

Ernie squeezed past her to get to the small kitchen area. "Oi, Chaz. Take a look through his wine selection, reckon there's a few here worth a bob or two." He inspected the water in the kettle, turned it on, and came out into the lounge while it boiled.

"Monroth was a dirty dealer in artworks of all sorts," he said. "If it was stolen, he could move it. If it hadn't been stolen, he knew people who could steal it for you. He'd authenticate fakes and denounce genuine articles. All that mattered to him was the price. If the price was right, Monroth was in."

Ernie sneered at the houseboat around them.

"You look at this place and you're thinking some low-down Thames-side Fagin character. Maybe that was what he became, but go back twenty years and he was working with the true power players. If the Saatchi's couldn't get you that colossal work of art for your corporate lobby then Vernon Monroth could. He was there at the biggest, the swankiest and the most debauched parties."

"Did he know Oxnard Pike?"

Ernie scratched his chin. "The art guy?" He shrugged. "There are different circles people move in. I do alright for meself but your Uncle Ernie don't get invited to the same parties as those one percenters. Vernon Monroth used to swim with the big sharks. He descended until he was swimming with a very different sort of predator." He tapped his own chest meaningfully.

The kettle clicked off. Ernie returned to the kitchen and rummaged in cupboards. Diana followed him.

"But, yeah," he said. "I reckon Vernon Monroth knew Oxnard Pike. Characters like Oxnard don't get where they are without treading on a few toes. Think on it. Oxnard's wealth is built on owning some of the most valuable works of art in the world. Think of the loans you can take out if you've got the Mona Lisa as collateral."

"He doesn't own the Mona Lisa, does he?"

Ernie laughed. "I don't know. Art's not my game. I know what I like. What's that one with the dogs playing cards?"

"Cassius Coolidge," said Chaz.

"I like that one," said Ernie.

There was a scurrying of tiny feet and the little terrier came dashing in. It weaved through the densely arranged furniture, leapt up onto a chair and sat in front of Diana, tail wagging as if insanely pleased with itself.

"That's a happy chap," said Ernie.

Diana reached out to stroke the handsome little dog. The terrier rubbed against her hand.

She scratched him under his collar and looked at the tag. *JMW Turner.*

"Turner? Is that your name?" she said.

The dog gave a yap.

"Dog named after a painter," she said.

"Maybe he's an artistic dog," suggested Chaz. "Does his own paintings?"

Ernie leaned round the doorway into the kitchen to give Chaz a questioning look.

"I've seen a chimp do paintings that sold for thousands," said Chaz.

"And Monroth would have been able to sell them," Ernie grunted.

Diana turned down the offer of a cup of tea and looked through Monroth's documents, hoping for glimmers of information. The lever arch folders of art information were intriguing but their purpose was unclear.

"Mind if I take these?" she said to Ernie, lifting the two folders.

The gangster shrugged. "Be my guest, Di."

Chaz had built up a small pile of effects and documents on the sofa. It didn't look like much. If Vernon Monroth was in debt to these two, it seemed unlikely they'd make back what they'd advanced.

She stepped out, walked up the short gangplank to the marina and then along to where Bertie had tied up.

"You alright?" he said, helping her aboard with her armfuls of folders.

"I think so."

"Ernie give you any trouble?"

She gave him a look. "Ernie is a teddy bear."

"Bear's about right. You know I said Sydney said the wrong thing to a bloke in the pub last night?"

"Yes?" She looked back at the houseboat. "You mean... Ernie?"

Bertie tried to smile. "Ernie's like an uncle to me. I love him. And he'll love you back, right up until the moment he don't."

"Is... is Sydney hurt?"

"Oh, just wounded pride." Bertie went to untie the boat.

"And his right wrist and three of his fingers. Is he coming with us?"

Diana turned to see the terrier, Turner, standing on the deck of Bertie's tug.

"No, he is not." She lifted the little dog onto the quayside.

Bertie went back to the wheelhouse, started the engines and pulled out into the marina and towards the Thames proper. Diana brought the lever arch files into the wheelhouse and put them down to look through them.

"What have you got there?" he asked.

"Files. Projects Vernon was working on maybe? A scrapbook?"

As she flicked through, she stopped at the sight of another postcard wedged between plastic wallets. It was yet another in the series of Butterfly Girls.

She flipped it over. The message was short and terse.

You're the one who killed him. You have more to lose than me.

"Crikey," she whispered.

There was a little bark. She looked round.

The terrier sat in the door to the wheelhouse, tail wagging at high speed.

"Oh, so you did decide to bring him with you after all," said Bertie.

CHAPTER THIRTY-NINE

"I CAN SEE A FISH!" Zaf cried. "No, wait, I can see loads!"

Now their descent had slowed, the swirling had resolved into a clearer picture. The Thames was a churning browny-grey for the most part but Zaf was surprised at what he could see.

So many fish. Some were chubby ovals, while others were tiny silvery flashes that switched direction in a split second. He looked down to the river's stony bed and saw a larger fish, grazing between strands of weed.

"You seem surprised," said Kamran.

"The Thames is all about boats and bridges for me," replied Zaf. "It never occurred to me there'd be fish, with it being so busy."

"The Thames was declared biologically dead in the fifties," said Faisal from his pilot's position.

"Dead?" said Zaf. "As in...?"

"Dead as a doornail," said Bev. "Unable to support life. All the pollution from the factories upstream. The Nazi bombing did terrible damage to the sewer system, too."

"But this?" Zaf waved a hand at the many fish going by.

"Decades of work to clean it up," said Bev.

"And it's now one of the cleanest city rivers in the world," added Faisal, "despite recent problems."

"There should be eels," said Bev. "Thames used to be full of 'em. I'd quite like to see an eel swimming by. Sandwich?"

She passed around the sandwiches as blithely as a grandma having a picnic on a beach. They all took one. Kamran asked Faisal to take their picture, for the adjudication later.

"These are very good, Bev," said Zaf. "I think your vinegar trick is a revelation."

"Sandwich, Faisal?" the old lady asked.

"If it's going to get eggy in here, then I might as well join in."

Zaf's eye was caught by something to the side. "Oh wow, is that an eel?"

Diana's mum looked. "It is! Good spot, Zaf."

Zaf found its movements fascinating. From the front it looked and swam like a fish, but then it had that long, snaky body behind, waving like a massive tail.

"You know about their lives?" asked Bev, between mouthfuls of egg sandwich.

Kamran and Zaf shook their heads.

"That eel there was born in the Sargasso Sea," she said. "That's Bermuda way, that is."

Zaf was intrigued.

"While they're still diddy," she continued, "they make the journey to Europe. They swim over four thousand miles and come up all the rivers to grow bigger. They can get into the tiniest bit of water, you wouldn't believe it. They get over obstacles, and even cross land if they need to."

"Is that for real?" Zaf said. "Have people seen them wriggling across their lawns or whatever?"

She shrugged. "I don't know about that, love, but they come in the rivers, grow into adults and then swim back to the Sargasso to have their own babies. You remember that, if you start thinking your life is hard. At least you're not an eel."

Kamran gave a hearty laugh and slapped his leg. "This is the best lunch I have had in a very long while. Beverley, you should be doing TED talks about how we should be inspired by eels."

"Who's Ted?" said Bev. "Another sarnie, anyone?"

CHAPTER FORTY

Mᴉɴᴅʏ, the receptionist at the Serenity Haven spa, was less than happy to see Diana coming in with a small dog on a makeshift string lead.

"This is a clean space," she said. "You ought to leave your dog at home."

"He's definitely not my dog," Diana replied. "I think Turner is very much his own dog."

"Turner? That's an unusual name for a dog."

"JMW Turner. You know? The painter?"

Mindy looked at the dog, then at Diana. Her gaze went back and forth. "He's a painter?"

No, thought Diana. *The real JMW Turner is more than a hundred and seventy years dead and this dog can't possibly be responsible for some of the most impressive romanticist paintings in the world.*

But she was feeling mischievous.

"Yes," said Diana. "He's very creative. And... he's my emotional support animal."

Mindy narrowed her eyes. "He wasn't with you previously."

"I wasn't as emotional then. And he was working on a piece in his studio."

Diana suppressed a snort. Surely Mindy would see through her teasing?

To her surprise, Mindy regarded Turner for a moment then waved them both through.

"I'll keep him under control," Diana assured her and went upstairs to call in on the temporary control room. She was keen to learn about progress on the sandwich challenge, and even keener to check that her mum was alright.

Robin was sitting at a big desk with many screens. "Hello, Diana. Can't stay away?" She caught sight of Turner and arched an eyebrow. "Hello. Who's this? Have you recently purchased a dog, Diana?"

"This is Turner. He's not mine."

"No? Whose is he?"

"If you must know, he belongs – belonged – to the man I saw fall off Oxnard's yacht."

Robin opened her mouth to speak, then simply smiled.

Turner sniffed around the room, pulling the lead to its fullest extent. Diana looked at the screens. "How are they all getting on?"

Robin picked out a monitor. "The live feed from your mother, Zaf and Kamran is off-air at the moment. They're in a submersible under the surface of the Thames."

Diana blinked. "What? Really?"

Robin nodded. "Kamran is working with a marine crew he's used many times, if that's a comfort."

Diana tapped her thigh with her fingertips. "They seemed alright as they were getting on, did they?"

"Your mum looked thrilled, to be honest. Zaf was hard to read, but I'd say he had a few reservations. Kamran was focused only on winning. They should be coming up any minute, so we'll see how they all are."

Diana looked across to the other monitors. "I can see Errol and Ariadne but I can't tell what they're doing. They don't look very happy, though."

"Right now, they're eating their sandwiches on a window cleaning rig outside the forty-fifth floor of a high rise in Canary Wharf," said Robin.

Diana felt the blood drain from her face. Perhaps it wasn't such a bad thing she'd been dismissed. "Oh. I see."

Robin raised an eyebrow. "I bet you're sorry you missed out on that."

Diana pulled back her shoulders. "I bet the views are amazing. Ariadne doesn't look as though she's admiring them. A shame."

"So that just leaves Oxnard, Alexsei and Nichola," said Robin. "Care to guess where they are?"

"Is that Nichola from Eccleston Square Gardens?" Diana said. "It is! Alexsei made a good call there. It looks like a massive stage or something. Is someone else there with... oh! Is that Bruce Springsteen?"

Robin nodded. "He's doing a sound check at the O2. They're eating their sandwiches onstage with Bruce Springsteen."

Diana widened her eyes. However Oxnard had managed to pull that off, she had to admit she was envious. "Incredible. I can't believe that this is just one year. I bet you've seen them pull some stunts over the years?"

"We had Kamran's party in a cage with a tiger one year."

"No! Surely that's not possible?"

"They were wheeled in there inside another cage that was supposed to protect them. I don't think it was a very comfortable experience. The cage had been constructed so the tiger couldn't get its paws inside, but it crushed the sides a little with its teeth. That tiger really wanted to snack on Kamran."

Diana shook her head. Money could remove barriers, but it seemed it could also remove common sense.

"There was the canteen at MI6 one time," Robin continued. "Oxnard had a contact who got them in. There have been abandoned underground stations and cupboards at the Palace of Westminster, too."

Diana nodded along.

Robin swivelled her chair to face Diana. "Where would you have suggested, if they'd asked you?"

Diana considered. "I know keyholders at some of the cemeteries. We could have had lunch in one of the catacombs."

"I think Oxnard did that in twenty-fifteen," said Robin. "Don't be constrained by things you could manage yourself. You've seen the doors their wealth will unlock."

"It's an eye-opener," said Diana. She really wasn't sure she wanted to be drawn into a world where such things were made possible by staggering amounts of money.

Having done all the sniffing he could, Turner turned in a little circle on the floor and lay down to sleep.

"Can I ask you something, Robin?" asked Diana.

"Of course."

"How did you get to be a valet to Tristram Ramsgate?"

Robin gave her look of suspicion. "Do you mean how does *one* get to be a valet? Or how did *I* get to be a valet?"

Diana shrugged. "It's an unusual career in this modern age."

Robin nodded. "I'm not sure if my parents ever understood

why I chose to do this. They both worked in hospitality, my father after a career in the RAF. Sent me to a private boarding school. I genuinely followed in my parents' footsteps, studied Hospitality Management at Surrey University. But I don't think they expected me to treat it as anything other than a way to broaden my horizons."

"No?"

Robin shook her head. "I'm not saying they thought I'd just bide my time in education until a wealthy husband came along. Or if they did, they never said it out loud. But they didn't expect me to take internships at Claridge's Hotel and then the Hurlingham Club. Oh, yes. The Hurlingham. I can swing a mean croquet mallet, let me tell you."

"A useful skill."

"And then I graduated and went straight into event management." Robin laughed. "It was at one of those events, I wasn't even twenty-three, that I met a young Tristram Ramsgate. Just come into his fortune as heir to a food and logistics empire. He was drunk. And he propositioned me."

Diana raised an eyebrow.

"Exactly!" Robin smiled. "A drunk rich guy asks a twenty-three-year-old woman if she'd like to be his valet. You're going to assume he's not *really* after a valet. I brushed him off. And then he made the same offer to me sober. You know what it was?"

"What?"

"Tristram was a man who never stopped. He built and built and worked. And when he came into his inheritance, he was presented with more than he could handle and it never occurred to him to slow down or back away. The night I met him, he was in the process of hiring everyone with an ounce of skill to help him manage what he now owned. He saw something in me, I don't know what. He thought he needed a valet and he thought the person he needed was me."

"You enjoyed working for him," said Diana. She could see the gleam in Robin's eyes.

"I loved the challenge. I loved the meticulousness of it. I love being that swan, all serene on the surface and paddling like hell underneath. I've got a killer poker face. I loved that Tristram never treated me as anything other than what I was – his valet. His wives, now ex-wives, saw that too. To him I was a sexless, genderless professional. I shouldn't have to state it but that was a real positive."

"Him dying must have been—"

"It was awful," said Robin with quiet ferocity. "You know how it happened?"

"I've heard snippets."

"The freeport storage facility. One more project than he needed. A failure in the fire safety system. The gas. How long can a person hold their breath?"

"A minute. Maybe two."

"Then that's how long it took him to die. At least that." She inhaled slowly through her nose. "But he saw I was taken care of after his death." She looked at Diana. "I'm a wealthy woman, Diana. Not even middle-aged and I never have to work again. I get to indulge in my passion projects, doing what little good I can."

There was a flicker, and the dead screen came to life. On the bobbing surface of the Thames, a hatch opened in a submarine. Diana couldn't help but be reminded of the Beatles.

"Your mother looks exhilarated," said Robin.

Diana watched her mum clamber out of the submarine onscreen. "I'm impressed."

"Yes?"

"If I recognise those buildings, then she's technically outside the bounds of the East End of London."

"That's impressive?"

"My mum would rather wrestle sharks in the Shadwell Basin than set a foot outside her manor."

"Wrestling sharks in Shadwell Basin," said Robin. "I'll make a note of that for next year's challenges."

CHAPTER FORTY-ONE

A T BEV'S INSISTENCE, Zaf had taken the spare sandwiches with him after dropping her off back home. Kamran sat in silence in the limo, basking in the satisfaction of a challenge well completed, the interior smelling gently of egg.

Diana stood in the reception of the spa holding a string lead with a little dog on the end of it. She smiled as she approached him. "You had fun today?"

Zaf shrugged. "It took a bit of getting used to, but honestly, it was an amazing experience."

"We will make an explorer of your friend yet," said Kamran, clasping Zaf on the shoulder before heading inside.

Zaf pointed at the dog. "You made a new friend."

"This is JMW Turner," she told him.

"The famous painter," added Mindy from behind the reception desk. Zaf looked at her: *What?*

JMW Turner barked as though he knew he was being talked about.

"Huh," said Zaf. "I'd expected him to be taller. Sandwich?"

He offered Diana a sandwich. She shook her head. "Do I detect a hint of vinegar?"

"Your mum swears by it. She's a character, isn't she?"

Diana smiled. "I've got something to show you. Perhaps we could go to *Tasty For You*. I'm sure Turner here will enjoy one of those sandwiches."

Diana was right. The little dog wolfed down a whole egg sandwich outside Levon's café before they went in.

"Is this your dog now?" Zaf asked.

As they ordered tea and cake, Diana told Zaf about her day: a ride on her cousin's boat, her encounter with Uncle Ernie, the connection with Vernon Monroth. Zaf had spent more than an hour in a submersible and he still felt jealous that he'd not got a ride on Diana's cousin's tugboat. But at least now he understood the terrier.

"So, this Vernon Monroth..." he said. "I don't get it. The guy on the boat received a bunch of postcards."

"They were among his things," said Diana as she pulled one out to show him.

It read, *You're the one who killed him. You have more to lose than me.*

"These are vintage postcards," said Diana. "They sell ones like them at that memorabilia shop in Cecil Court. Vernon Monroth was an art dealer, a crooked one. Big Ernie says he'd authenticate fakes or denounce a genuine article as a forgery if there was money in it. And it seems likely he knew Oxnard."

"OK," said Zaf, digesting what she'd told him. "So Oxnard is basically a high-end art dealer. He owns works of art. It's no different from hoarding gold or jewels. They were in the same business."

Levon brought the tea in a battered enamel pot, along with

a selection of fondant-covered cakes on a plate. Diana thanked him and they both waited until he was gone.

"So," she said, "Vernon had been receiving postcards. He had some of them on him when I bumped into him below the London Eye. There were these others in his houseboat."

She placed the other one in front of Zaf. He leaned in to read.

We will discuss your demands. 11am next Tuesday. The Silver Salmon. *Moored at London County Hall.*

"Oxnard's yacht," he said. "The exact time and place you saw him."

Diana nodded. "We have a series of communications. Unsigned, anonymous. The sender mentions the other person's demands. The sender says the recipient is 'as much to blame'."

Zaf looked up from the card. "Vernon Monroth was blackmailing someone."

"My thoughts exactly."

"And if it's an invitation to Oxnard's yacht then the most obvious conclusion is that it's Oxnard being blackmailed."

"The most obvious, indeed," agreed Diana. She sliced one of the cakes in two and took a bite.

Zaf watched her. *Always so cool.* "And if we're talking about someone being responsible for someone else's death... then I'm thinking of Tristram Ramsgate."

Diana nodded. "Killed by halon gas in a supposed accident."

He poured for both of them, his mind racing. The tea was a rich bronze colour.

He put the pot down. "No," he said.

She frowned. "No?"

"It all makes sense of a sort except... OK, so either Vernon or Oxnard or both of them were responsible for Tristram's death. I don't know how. They hold that knowledge over each other for years, and then this Vernon guy, who sounds kind of creepy, decides he wants a bit of what Oxnard's got and blackmails him. Except Oxnard is having none of that so he invites Vernon to his boat and – bam! – kills him and tosses him overboard. It all makes sense except—"

"Oxnard was standing right next to us in the London Eye when it happened."

"Yeah. As alibis go, that's pretty watertight."

Diana pulled a face. "You're right."

Zaf shrugged. "He could have hired a hit man."

"A paid assassin?"

"These guys are super-wealthy."

Diana shook her head. "Then why would Oxnard invite him to the yacht? If you're going to pay someone to kill a person, surely you'd get them to do it somewhere quiet. Vernon's houseboat would have fit the bill perfectly. No. It doesn't quite work."

Zaf added milk to their cups. "You're right. It's a pain, but you are."

She reached down to the bag at her side. "It was this I really wanted to show you."

She set down two grubby lever arch files on the table, making two *thuds*. Little Turner twitched on the floor.

"These were in Vernon Monroth's houseboat," she said.

Zaf eased one open. "You stole these?"

She gave him a look. "The man is dead and no one else seems to care. I'm *borrowing* them."

Zaf flicked through the folder. Page after page, wallet after wallet, was devoted to documents and information relating to individual pieces of art. *View of Auvers-sur-Oise* by Cézanne,

The Swallow by Marie Bacquemond, *Portrait of Winston Churchill* by Graham Sutherland...

"What is this?" he asked.

"I thought you could tell me, Mr Art History degree."

He felt a twitch in his cheek, the one he got whenever he spoke to his mum about what he was doing these days. "*Failed* Art History degree," he said. He paused on the Churchill painting, the elderly politician portrayed in drab browns and greys. "This one's familiar."

"Was Vernon Monroth doing research?"

Zaf shrugged. "There's nothing much to link these. Impressionists, modernists. It's not like this is research for a book or something."

He slurped his tea, musing. There was something familiar about it all, but he couldn't put his finger on it.

"Maybe Vernon Monroth was buying them for a client, or maybe he was selling them," suggested Diana.

"Some of these are priceless," said Zaf. "This is a Renoir. I couldn't even tell you how much this would be worth. Maybe Oxnard would know."

Diana shook her head. "I think we should keep this between ourselves for now. Until we know what's going on."

CHAPTER FORTY-TWO

Within half an hour they were back at the spa for the adjudication of the day's challenge. Zaf felt pride in what he'd achieved, and was looking forward to seeing the footage.

"Excellent, we're all here," said Robin. "It's time for the adjudication."

The three men smiled at each other. Each exuded satisfaction. They'd all done something impressive, Zaf reckoned, something they thought deserved to win. The three helpers plus Diana sat at the foot of the table. Zaf tried to ignore the way Diana refused to meet Ariadne's eye.

"A brief slideshow will accompany my commentary," said Robin, "but as always, I will edit together a lengthier version for you to enjoy later."

Zaf could imagine them in their island paradises or ski lodges, playing their greatest hits when they were bored. Men who craved novelty the way these three did must get bored quite often.

"Let us start with an overview of Errol's activities," Robin continued. "This picture shows the team being kitted out with hard hats and having a safety briefing, before stepping into the window-cleaning cradle that was to be their base for the next hour or so. Here they are, having reached floor forty-five. You can see by their expressions that the environment has altered."

"It was damn windy," said Ariadne with a raised eyebrow. "Lucky the ACE Tours uniform is made from pure new wool. If I'd been in polyester, I'd have frozen to death up there."

Zaf could imagine an hour in that tiny cradle, so high above the ground, swaying in the wind and looking down at the void beneath your feet. He glanced at Diana, who was still gazing ahead, not reacting to Ariadne's comments.

"Well," said Robin, "you both ate a sandwich and made it back down to the ground, so the rules were satisfied. Let's move onto Oxnard's entry, shall we?"

Oxnard exchanged a smile with Alexsei. Oxnard was dressed in his usual outfit, and had probably been wearing the same thing since before Zaf was born. But Alexsei was in a t-shirt Zaf hadn't seen before. Maybe he'd ruined his clothes or got a soaking. Zaf hoped his boyfriend's day hadn't been as awful as his visions of that cradle.

"Here's a picture showing the group. You will see that they have a guest, called Nichola, who was born within the sound of Bow Bells. The three of them can be seen here outside the O2 arena."

Robin displayed another slide.

"Here they are on stage while Bruce Springsteen does his sound check, eating their egg sandwiches."

There were gasps of surprise around the room. The picture captured the trio next to the rock legend himself, immersed in his sound check and ignoring the picnickers. Another picture flashed up with Oxnard shaking Bruce's hand and looking to camera with a triumphant grin.

"You old dog," said Kamran. "Do you even *like* rock music? I thought you only listened to classical."

Oxnard inspected his fingernails with studied nonchalance. "As I always say, if you're going to listen to something loud and brash, then you might as well go all-in. I do have a soft spot for The Boss, and when I realised he was playing here during our challenge I couldn't resist."

"On we go to Kamran's entry," said Robin. "Here we have some pictures of the sandwiches being made. It's not often we have a window into that part of the day, but Beverley Bakewell was quite insistent that she take on the task."

Zaf hoped no one would comment on Bev's tiny kitchen with its worn decor, but the billionaires seemed mildly fascinated by it. He thought he saw a small twist of mockery on Ariadne's face, but she had the sense to keep her mouth closed.

"Now here's a picture showing the team next to their venue for the challenge. It's a submersible, shown above water here." Robin clicked through. "Here they all are eating their sandwiches below the surface of the river Thames."

There were appreciative noises from around the room. But who would win? Zaf had discounted the window cleaning rig. It was crazy, but it didn't have the 'wow' factor of the other two.

Robin sat back with a smile, waiting for the hubbub to die down. "It is now time for me to determine who our winner will be. As you know, I assess each entry as follows." She counted off on her fingers. "How impossible and inaccessible does it seem? How did you approach it, and exploit any opportunities that came your way? And finally, how impactful is it? Does it knock my socks off?"

Zaf held his breath. *The submersible, surely...*

Robin surveyed the group. "I have received a written submission from each of you, detailing your preparations.

Based upon all of the evidence I have seen, I pronounce the winner of this task to be Oxnard."

Zaf felt his shoulders slump. Oxnard gave a modest bow of his head, while Alexsei punched the air and stood to show them the back of his t-shirt. It listed the dates for the current Bruce Springsteen tour, but he'd used marker pen to add *Oxnard, Alexsei and Nichola* to the London date.

There was a polite round of applause, but Errol looked less than pleased.

CHAPTER FORTY-THREE

DIANA TRIED NOT to indulge in *schadenfreude*, but she had to work hard to avoid looking over at Ariadne, who'd been eclipsed by the other two entries. It might have been Diana in the same place, but she'd been swapped out.

She wasn't sorry.

"Ladies and gents," said Errol. "I would like you all to be my guests for a luxury dining experience this evening. Chef has been working hard on some exquisite new dishes. Dinner will be in around ninety minutes, and in the meantime if you would like to use the spa's amenities, then please do. It is all at your disposal."

Diana exchanged glances with Zaf and they left the room together. They wandered through the spa building, curious about the treatments on offer. Mindy in reception smiled as Diana asked about the options.

"What kind of treatment were you looking for?" she asked.

"I was going to look at the list and then decide."

The receptionist consulted the computer moulded into the desk. "Our therapists are multi-disciplinary experts in delivering holistic solutions. If you have no specific problem areas to address, perhaps you are looking for a facial or a massage?"

"That sounds nice," said Diana. "Yes, a facial I think."

"I always enjoy a facial," said Zaf.

"Sculpting, nurturing, elevating or purging?" asked Mindy.

Diana was taken aback by the mumbo-jumbo. "Did you say purging?"

"Sounds a bit harsh," said Zaf.

"Oh, no," said Mindy with a fake laugh. "Our purging treatments use our range of aura cleansing lotions. They gently burn away—"

"Burn?" asked Diana.

"Gently, apparently," added Zaf.

"Gently burn away the old, haggard you," said Mindy, "leaving only the better, fresher you that we all know and love."

On the floor, Turner barked.

"It's not suitable for dogs," Mindy added.

Zaf gripped Diana's arm. She turned to find him looking into her eyes, his expression grave.

"I know," he said. "I know where I've seen that painting." He glanced at Mindy. "Excuse us a minute."

"Another time, perhaps," said Diana. She had little interest in purging treatments, no matter how gently they burned.

Zaf pulled her away to a low glass table and urged her to get out the folder of art pictures. She had to bat his hands away before they could get the folder out and open.

"I knew I knew that Churchill picture. It was on *The Crown*."

"*The Crown*?"

"The TV show. You know, about the Queen."

"This isn't really Art History degree knowledge, is it?"

He pouted. "Thing is, it was in one of the episodes." He

found the painting in the folder. "This man Sutherland painted it, but Churchill absolutely hated it."

Diana could see why. While the painting was masterful and characterful, it was really quite unflattering to the former Prime Minister. It showed him slouched and scowling, in a state of confusion.

"He hated it so much that it was burned," said Zaf. "His wife or secretary or someone. They just took it out and burned it. So the story goes."

"Ah," said Diana. "Burning away the old and haggard."

"Anyway," said Zaf, "once I remembered that, I recalled the Renoir in here." He flicked back to a folder entitled '*Landscape with Two People* by Renoir'. "This *is* Art History knowledge. Look." The picture he was pointing at was a blurry fragment of an image. "This is actually from a painting by another artist. Um, Bazille or Manet or someone."

"Sorry?" said Diana. "I don't follow you?"

Zaf tapped the image. "Renoir painted a picture. *Landscape with Two People*. But *this* image comes from another painting. It's an image of an artist's studio with pictures on the wall. The only reason we know *Landscape with Two People* ever existed is because it appears in another painting. This one. The actual *Landscape* was lost. No one knows where it is."

"A painting within a painting."

Zaf nodded. "The thing the Churchill picture and this Renoir have in common is that they no longer exist. Or what's what we assume." He riffled through the other pages. "These other pictures. I would have to check, but it's possible the one thing they all have in common—"

"Is that they don't exist?"

"I don't know why an art dealer would be interested in such things."

"I don't either," said Diana, but an idea was starting to form in her mind. Part of her felt as if she was approaching something, a glimpse of the whole piece.

She checked her watch. "I need to visit the memorabilia shop again. It should still be open." She looked down at the little dog, still on its lead. "Would you mind taking Turner here for a little walk?"

"Me?" said Zaf.

"I'll try to be back as quick as I can."

Diana hurried out of the spa and turned right, in the direction of Baker Street underground.

"Do we own a dog now?" Zaf called after her.

CHAPTER FORTY-FOUR

Diana raced away from the spa, not answering Zaf's question. Zaf looked down at the dog. The dog looked up at him.

Turner was one of those dogs who wore a constant expression of expectation. *What now? Are we going to do the thing? Are we doing it now?*

The only problem was, Zaf had no idea what *the thing* was.

He tried a guess. "OK," he said to the dog. "A walk once round the block and that's it."

Turner responded with a little yap.

"Off out?" called Alexsei, coming into reception.

"Just me and my little doggy," replied Zaf.

"You have a dog now?"

"It has been a weird week."

"It will be over soon. Would you like company on your walk?"

Zaf eyed Alexsei's T-shirt. "You might be a bit cold going out like that."

Alexsei smiled. "Then maybe you will have to keep me warm."

Zaf held out an arm, ready to pull Alexsei in a hug, as a door banged open and a frizzy-haired woman in the spa's uniform came storming into the reception area, a phone pressed to her ear.

Alexsei nuzzled up to Zaf. "More drama," he whispered.

Zaf raised an eyebrow.

The woman bent behind the reception counter, seemingly looking for something. She moved past Alexsei and Zaf to search the lobby, pulling the leaves of glossy plants to one side and peering under the plush sofas.

"No, not in here," she said into the phone. "I don't care if it's a Manolo. I can't see it."

She banged back through the door and disappeared.

Mindy had been standing behind the reception desk throughout the incident, ignored by the woman. Zaf gave her a questioning look.

"I do apologise for that," she said with exaggerated calm. "A little speedbump on our road towards inner harmony."

"What's a Manolo?" asked Alexsei.

"It's a kind of shoe," said Zaf. He stopped. "Oh, my..."

"What is it?"

Zaf released Alexsei and hurried outside onto the pavement. The noise of evening traffic, the sounds of London, filled the air. He looked up and down the road and then at the buildings on the other side of the road.

Alexsei was behind him. "What is it?"

Zaf turned to him. "Shoes."

"What?"

Zaf crossed the road. The spa was on Manchester Road.

The next road over was Chiltern Street. Which meant the Chartwell and Crouch depot was a stone's throw away.

He looked up at the rear of the building in front of them. There was a fire door set into it and nothing else of note. He peered at the edges of the building, at the sliver of a passageway separating it from the next building. Turner pulled at his lead and sniffed at a drainpipe.

"What are you doing?" asked Alexsei, crossing after him.

"I'm looking for a way in."

"A way in?"

Zaf nodded. "We've got this problem in the depot. Gus keeps stealing shoes."

"Gus the cat?"

"He's the only Gus I know. And I couldn't work it out. *We* couldn't work it out. It was single shoes. Lefts and rights. And they were all really classy shoes, I mean super expensive. It was like he'd been sneaking into a shoe shop or something. Because where else would super expensive shoes be left lying around?"

"The changing rooms of a super expensive spa gym?"

"Well, yeah." Zaf held Turner's lead out for Alexsei to take, and dashed back into the spa. He slammed into the reception desk in his excitement.

"Hey, Mindy," he said. "By any chance, have some of your customers' shoes been going missing lately?"

Mindy's smile dropped. "No, sir. I don't know what you've heard but we treat our clients' belongings with the same care we would treat our own."

"Are you sure?"

"I am very sure."

"So not a Manolo. Or that Salvatore Ferragamo I heard someone shouting about the other day?"

"I'm sure I don't know what you mean. And any instances of theft that may or may not have occurred have already been reported to the police. Is there anything else I can help you with?"

"You have been more than helpful," Zaf assured her. He hurried out again.

Alexsei was standing in the pavement, Turner looking up at him with a *what about my walk?* expression. "I am not sure what is occurring," he said.

"Gus is stealing shoes from the spa," said Zaf. He put his arm through Alexsei's and pulled him close. "Now, let's take Turner for a turn round the block and work out what to do about it."

CHAPTER FORTY-FIVE

DIANA WAS in a hurry to get to Stanley Grosvenor Memorabilia. So she was pleasantly surprised to find a train on the platform when she arrived at Baker Street tube station. Twenty minutes later, she was at Charing Cross and in the alleyway housing the shop. The dusty yellow light still streaming from shop windows and the occasional carriage lamp jutting out from the walls elevated the charm of the narrow street.

The lights were on in the memorabilia shop and the bell jangled as she entered.

"Closing in fifteen minutes," said Old Philbin before looking up and recognising Diana. He pointed a crooked finger at her, frowning. "We've met before," he said.

"I was in here earlier this week," she said. "With Mr Dadashov, Mr Pike and Mr van Blerk."

"Yes, you were," said Philbin, eyes lighting up. "And you were enquiring after the Schmucker postcards."

"Well remembered," she said.

"But I don't recall your name."

"Diana Bakewell. I've actually come to ask about the postcards again."

She dropped the two postcards she had on the counter. Philbin brushed the images of the Art Nouveau butterfly girls with his fingertips.

"Oh," he said. "Selling, not buying."

"I've just got questions," she told him. "These were part of a set. Several postcards."

"Not common to find them together. Old Philbin was lucky enough to come across a box of them. Unused, unsent."

He flipped one over and tsked to see writing and a stamp on the reverse.

"I hoped you might say that," Diana said. "I wondered... if someone had bought a whole set of these, might you know about it?"

Without a word, he moved along the counter and consulted a dusty accounting ledger. Old Philbin had clearly not moved into the twenty-first century.

"I appreciate you might not be comfortable with divulging customer details," she said.

"Old Philbin can look. He doesn't have to tell." The white-haired man licked a finger and turned a page. "I sell odd ones here and there. But a set... Hmmm..." He turned another page. "Ah."

"Ah?" Diana could feel her heart racing.

He tapped the page. "Ordered for delivery. Brooke Mansion, Hampstead Lane, Highgate."

"That's the address? The customer details aren't on there?"

Philbin looked up, shaking his head. "You could always go knock on the door and find out."

"Thank you," she said. "That's really helpful."

Diana made for the door, pausing as a thought occurred to her.

"You're a dealer in art," she said.

Philbin smiled and spread his thin arms. "Curios, knick-knacks and memories."

"Can you think of a reason why anyone would be interested in works of art that had gone missing? I mean, commercially."

"Missing how?"

"Like, er, this one by Renoir. Landscape with two figures. It's these two women..."

"Ah, *Paysage avec deux personnages*," said Philbin. "I know it. It's not *all* missing. A portion of it exists, but the rest is lost. Missing art. I understand. Do you like magic tricks?"

"Pardon?"

Old Philbin opened a glass-topped box on the shop counter and removed a coin. He held it between gnarly fingertips.

"Art – even knick-knacks and memories such as the items I own – lives two lives. There is the art itself, the thing of beauty and..." He turned the coin around from head to tails. "There's the item of value. There is art all around us, but only some of it has monetary worth. And then some of that art goes missing."

A twist of the wrist and the coin disappeared, dropped into his hand or a sleeve.

"We can only appreciate the individual work of art if we can actually experience it, see it. But the value of the artwork remains, whether it is locked away in some oil prince's secret gallery or forgotten in a Swiss bank vault. It exists. It has value."

His fingers flickered and the coin appeared in the other hand.

"And sometimes the art resurfaces and the world can

glimpse it again for a while. Sometimes, it is discovered to be a forgery." The coin vanished once more. "The very reality of individual art changes with the decades and centuries."

Diana cocked her head. "But you can't own something that isn't there."

"Ha! Old Philbin begs to differ." The old man cackled and rolled the coin around in his hand. "The Yapese people of Micronesia made their coins from carved stone, stone disks with little holes in the middle. They traded them."

"Is that so?"

"And the people of the Yap islands made bigger and bigger coins. The size of the coin denoted its value. Colossal stones, eight feet across, were markers of great wealth. Big stone, big value. These huge stones were almost too heavy to move, once made. You couldn't take them to the shops to buy your groceries. And there's one stone, huge, that when they tried to move it, it rolled down the hill, off the cliff and into the harbour. Sploosh!"

"Lost artwork," she said.

"Precisely. But did the owner of that stone disk lose the value attached to it? No. Everyone knew it was there, some-where under the water. So the value remained. And when the owner traded it – to buy a bigger hut, I don't know – then everyone knew the sunken stone coin had a new owner."

Diana grunted in understanding. "Art has value even if you can't access it."

"You can buy shares, like stock market shares, in artwork. You can take out loans against them. You can even buy art 'futures', the promise to buy art at a fixed price in the future." He turned the coin in his hand, from tails to heads. "Old Philbin is more interested in the beauty of a thing. A Queen Anne half-crown, a piece of history, its value incidental."

He returned his coin to the box on the counter and closed the lid.

"You have been remarkably helpful," said Diana.

CHAPTER FORTY-SIX

BACK AT THE SPA, and still accorded the privileges of a guest despite being dropped as Errol van Blerk's helper, Diana changed into a dress made from plum-coloured silk and decorated with an extravagant number of black dropper beads. It always made her feel as if she was about to board the Orient Express. She found the other guests in the dining room.

The starter was a cucumber and mint gazpacho. As she sipped the cool soup, she leaned over to Zaf.

"You don't have the dog?"

"Turner is at the depot. I made him a little bed in the kitchen."

"How did Gus take to that? Having a dog in his domain?"

"He went and sulked in the rafters somewhere. In fact, I've got some news to share about Gus, the thief of ladies' shoes."

"Oh?"

Before Zaf had a chance to explain he was interrupted by Kamran, leaning across the table to speak to her. "You dodged a bullet today, I think," he said.

"A bullet?" she asked.

"I would not think it was pleasant up high on that window cleaner's cradle, no?"

Ariadne was further down, sitting by Errol, wearing a knee-length navy blue dress with a modest neckline topped with a delicate silver necklace and matching earrings. The elegant outfit had failed to completely obliterate her look of windswept shock.

Diana permitted herself a small smile. "Yes. Perhaps I did."

"I would poach you for myself," said Kamran, "but your colleague brings his own uniqueness to these challenges."

"I'm game for anything," said Zaf. "By the way, this soup is *meant* to be cold, right?"

She smiled. Gazpacho, Zaf. Yes."

He raised an eyebrow. "Good. I like it."

The main course was Mediterranean chicken accompanied by lemon and herb-infused couscous. As the group set to eating it, Diana turned to Zaf.

"What was it you were going to tell me about Gus?" she asked.

"He's been..." He looked around the table, his gaze snagging on Alexsei. "I'll tell you later."

"I hope he hasn't got us into trouble."

Zaf said nothing, but shrugged then cleared his throat. "Any joy at the postcard shop?"

"Mmmm." She lowered her voice. "I've got a lead on the postcards."

Listening to her, Zaf misfed a forkful of sauce-covered peppers into his mouth. He put his fork down and looked for his napkin.

Alexsei reached over with his own napkin and wiped sauce from Zaf's cheek. Zaf smiled back into his eyes.

"Ha! I knew it," said Ariadne.

The three competitors looked up.

"Oh, come on," said Ariadne. "They obviously make an adorable couple."

Diana felt Zaf tense beside her. He and Alexsei both looked stricken, as though caught out doing something wrong.

"Dad..." Alexsei began.

Zaf put a hand on Alexsei's arm. Then he looked directly at Kamran. "We're a couple, Mr Dadashov," he said. "We were going to tell you afterwards." He glanced at Alexsei. "We *are* describing ourselves as a couple, aren't we?"

Alexsei gave a small nod. "I mean... yes? I wasn't thinking we were anything else."

"Oh, me neither. Very much a couple." Zaf wrinkled his nose. "Yes, Mr Dadashov. We're a couple."

Diana looked at Kamran. His face was blank.

"So," he said to Zaf, "my son has not only formed a partnership with you, but has brought us into each other's company? It is an unusual introduction."

Zaf's smile had dropped. "Yes, sir. Hello."

Diana watched him, proud of her young colleague. He wasn't wilting under Kamran's scrutiny, as she imagined many others would have in the past. She noticed Zaf and Alexsei leaning unconsciously towards each other while facing Kamran, as though covertly seeking support.

Oxnard snorted. "He kept that quiet. It's scandalous on so many levels."

"Scandalous, Oxnard?" said Kamran.

A nod. "I want to lodge a complaint, Robin."

"Against young love?" asked Robin.

Oxnard shook his head. "In terms of the Tradition. The challenges. There's an obvious conflict of interest here—"

"Oh, do shut up Oxnard," said Errol, "this isn't about you."

Kamran was still staring at Alexsei and Zaf.

"Did I speak out of turn?" said Ariadne. Diana wished she was closer, so she could kick the woman under the table.

"No," said Kamran. He flung an arm out at the young men. "It is these two who should have spoken up sooner."

"Father," said Alexsei, "I didn't want to distract you from your week and—"

"It is tremendous news!" Kamran clapped his hands, stood and addressed Alexsei and Zaf with open arms. "I am very happy for you both, and I want you to give me a hug this instant!"

Zaf and Alexsei exchanged glances, then made their way around the table to embrace Kamran. Diana could feel the relief pouring off them as they grinned at each other.

Kamran pulled back, looking into the eyes of each of the young men in turn. "Somebody bring Champagne! This calls for a celebration."

CHAPTER FORTY-SEVEN

ZAF COULD FEEL A ROARING, pounding exhilaration inside him. Kamran Dadashov had embraced him, both metaphorically and literally. Zaf didn't give two hoots about seeking parental approval for his romantic choices, but now it was all out in the open, the weird formality between him and Alexsei that had marked the week could be dropped.

The two of them took the final bottle of Champagne up to the rooftop garden. Night had settled but the streetlights of the city cast a yellow light over everything and gave shape to the darkness. Soft solar lights made oases of the different screened-off sections of the garden.

Alexsei topped up Zaf's glass. "And now we can be us again," he said.

"Amen to that."

Alexsei kissed him. "You seriously asked if the gazpacho was meant to be cold?"

"It was a joke," said Zaf. "A joke. I'm not entirely uncultured."

"Oh, he is a most intelligent young man, I think," said Kamran, stepping into the circle of light by their seats.

Zaf sprang to his feet. "Mr Dadashov."

The older man smiled. His smile was as handsome as his son's.

"It was Kamran before," he said. "It is Kamran now. No need for this 'Mr Dadashov'. I wonder if I might speak to my son."

"No. Of course, of course. Kamran."

Kamran slapped Zaf on the shoulder and Zaf retreated to let them talk.

"Why did you hide him away from me?" Kamran began. "You think I would not approve?"

Zaf resisted the urge to listen in and was out of earshot before Alexsei replied. He retreated to a garden area where Diana was standing looking out over the rooftops.

"I think that went as well as it could," she said.

"The meal?" he asked.

She gestured towards Alexsei and Kamran. "Your introduction to the family."

Zaf smiled. "We're not about to go looking for wedding venues or anything. We've not been going out long."

"It's never too early to meet the family. You said you had news about Gus and the shoe thefts."

"Ah, yes," said Zaf. "The shoes are coming from here." He pointed. "The depot isn't far away, if you go via the route a cat would take. It explains the odd shoes."

She shook her head. "Gus is stealing the shoes. From here."

"Changing rooms. Therapy rooms. He's sneaking in somewhere and stealing designer shoes when no one's looking. The spa is trying to keep it hush-hush."

"Well, knowing where they've come from is half the

battle," she said. "How to repatriate them without something daft happening again, like Newton getting arrested, that's the trickier part."

He nodded. "You said you had found a lead of your own."

"The postcards Vernon Monroth was sent. There's a good chance they were all bought from that memorabilia shop. The owner had an address for someone who bought a whole batch of them. Brooke Mansion on Hampstead Lane. If we're lucky we can... Are you OK?"

She stopped, looking into his face. Her words had sparked off a recollection in his mind. He just needed to make the connections.

"I know that address," he said.

"Know it as in...? It's a pricey corner of London. Every house probably worth a hundred times what either of us make in a year."

"One and a half times," Zaf muttered, the memory returning to him. "The House Swap gambit."

"What?"

"Robin and I were talking about the postcard challenge and... Yes. Oxnard."

"Oxnard?"

"She told me. That's where Oxnard lives. Brooke Mansion. That's Oxnard's address."

Diana's mouth widened. "Oxnard bought the postcards. I mean, it shouldn't surprise me. And yet it does."

Zaf nodded, thinking. "Vernon and Oxnard knew each other in the past. That's definite. Vernon was blackmailing someone and, if the victim was writing his replies on those postcards, then that person was Oxnard." He stared into her eyes. "Vernon was blackmailing Oxnard over their shared involvement in someone's death. Which... which would have been Tristram Ramsgate, fifteen years ago. It all fits."

"Except for the vital thing," said Diana. "The problem we've already spotted."

He felt his body slump. He couldn't be wrong, surely. But...

"When Vernon died," he said, "Oxnard was with us. Hundreds of feet in the air in a sealed glass pod. Yeah. That is a tricky one."

They stopped talking as voices approached across the rooftop.

"... of course, it is a surprise. But I know enough from my relationship with your *baba* Dadashov and from the marriage I had to your mother... we cannot live other people's lives for them."

"I'm so relieved," Alexsei replied. "I thought... I thought you had plans for me."

"The only plan I have is to protect you," Kamran said as they stepped into the light close to Diana and Zaf. "We will do anything to protect and honour those we love." His gaze shifted to Zaf. "Is that not so?"

"Love is a powerful motivator," Diana agreed.

"Come now," said Kamran. "It is late. Tomorrow, the greatest of the three challenges awaits us all."

CHAPTER FORTY-EIGHT

DIANA SPENT another night in the guest bedroom at the spa. Her dreams were of Vernon Monroth. In those dreams, the man was creeping along empty corridors, from light to shadow to light again. He moved on creeping tiptoes. She could not tell if he was alive or dead, if he was creeping up on someone or trying to creep away. But he never stopped. He was a restless and unhappy soul and would find no peace.

She rose early and went over to the depot to check on the dog who seemed to have become her responsibility. JMW Turner was happily sniffing around the kitchen, but hadn't caused any destruction or mess in the night.

Gus was in the depot proper, curled up on the bonnet of one of the beautiful Routemaster buses and glaring at the kitchen door, fully aware of the little dog that had spent the night behind it.

"I don't have a huge amount of sympathy for you today," she told the cat. "Stealing shoes from the ladies at the spa. Really?"

Gus turned his face away, pretending not to hear.

Diana took the dog for a walk around the block before returning to the Serenity Haven spa. After breakfast there was a briefing from Robin Silversmith. Diana sat at the back, watching everyone's expressions. She was no longer Errol van Blerk's helper but she was keen to stick with the group.

"I will run through the rules for the final challenge, known only as The Race," said Robin. "The start and finish of the race will be drawn from a list of locations. Competitors must travel between these points in the shortest time possible, accompanied by their assistant. The means of transport is entirely up to you, as long as you stick to the following rules. Contestants' own feet or footwear may not touch the ground, they may not use the regular public transport infrastructure and finally, if their chosen transport method uses an internal combustion engine, then it should date from before nineteen-seventy."

Zaf raised his hand. "Can we get other people to help with this challenge?"

"Yes," said Robin. "There is currently no limit on the number of extra helpers. Of course, if I need to modify the rules for future events, that may change. Clear?"

Zaf nodded.

"Now, there are a couple of other things that you need to know. The results of the other two challenges play into this. So the winners of each of the other challenges gets sixty seconds knocked off their time for today's challenge. This is obviously an advantage for Mr Pike and Mr Dadashov, but it doesn't mean that Mr van Blerk is out of the running. The winner of today's challenge is the overall winner and it could be any one of you. If I see any evidence of law-breaking, inconveniencing the public or obvious sabotage, I will apply a sixty-second time penalty to the perpetrator. This is entirely at my discretion and it's the rule that I hope will keep your efforts honourable."

There were nods around the room.

"Let's move on to the draw, where we will decide the start and finish." Robin projected a map onto one of the displays. "We are looking at the Circle and District lines, the Central line and the Northern line. They have been chosen because they represent a good set of locations within central London. We have removed the stations at the extremities of those lines, and so we will draw from this set of possibilities."

She brought out a vintage top hat. "I will invite Diana to draw the station that will be the start of our journey."

Robin walked across the room and held out the hat.

Diana picked out a slip of paper and Robin gestured for her to open it up.

"The start of the race will be Waterloo," said Diana.

"Thank you, Diana. Waterloo is a large station, and I suggest that you begin near to the taxi rank. Now we will select a finish. If we pull out a station that is three stops or fewer from Waterloo then we will discard it. Can I please ask you to pull out a second slip, Diana? You are unaffiliated."

Diana reached in again. "Hammersmith." She handed the slips to Robin.

Waterloo to Hammersmith was about five miles across London. It would be a half-hour journey along the Circle Line, maybe forty minutes by taxi. But neither option would be available to competitors, given they were not permitted to use either public transport or modern vehicles.

"There you have it," said Robin. "You will wear the body-cams as before and I will monitor progress from here."

The room was alive with muttered conversations, as each of the participants turned to their helper.

"You are very welcome to spend some time in here, Diana," said Robin.

Diana smiled. "I might do that, thank you."

There was a beep from her phone. A text had come through.

Call me. We need to talk. DCI Sugarbrook.

Diana hit dial.

CHAPTER FORTY-NINE

SUGARBROOK'S NUMBER went straight to voicemail. Diana tried again and it did exactly the same.

The competitors were beginning to leave the room. There was much urgent discussion as they left, mainly the issuing of instructions.

As the room emptied of all participants other than herself and Robin, Diana moved forward to see some of the information displays. She kept pressing call for Sugarbrook but to no avail.

"I guess this is a challenge where they can prepare their approach in advance," she said to Robin. "There perhaps isn't so much input from the helpers."

"You'd be surprised," said Robin. "The unknown element is always where the journey is. How long will it be, and what sort of places are they? The only one who has a completely pre-prepared approach is Kamran. Do you see how he's typing into a tablet? Well, he ran a series of tests and had someone build him a computer programme to help with this challenge."

"How does that help?"

"It's a simulation predicting the success of a range of transport options for a given journey. For example, I believe it favours human-powered transport options for very short distances."

"Human-powered," said Diana. "If they were pushed in a wheelchair?"

"Wheelchair, sedan chair, piggyback. Kamran has tested them all. He hasn't made the results known to the others, obviously. The advantage of zero equipment is that they can get to Waterloo and get started very quickly if they don't have to wait around for a conveyance."

"Waterloo to Hammersmith is a bit far for a piggyback, though."

Robin nodded.

The webcam feeds showed the groups heading out and into the road. Motorbikes waited for them and they all sped off into the traffic.

"They can use any means they like to get to the start," said Robin. "The tube's normally the fastest, but they all seem to have decided that a motorbike is the best option from here. But I will be looking out for anyone who drives on pavements or endangers pedestrians."

A few minutes of watching the feed dipping and swooping was enough for Diana. As they arrived outside the station each group found a group of people awaiting them.

"Good grief," she said to Robin, "they look like a Formula 1 pit crew or something."

A smile. "Each of them will want to make sure that whatever they are using has the best route, and a good support team all the way along it. They will be in touch through those radio mikes they are all wearing."

"It's a shame we can't hear everything they're saying."

Robin tapped her earpiece. "Oh, I'm getting it all. But I might not share until the recorded highlights are put together."

Diana raised an eyebrow. "Recorded highlights, huh?"

"They get together over the festive period and watch reruns. The production quality goes up every year. They take it very seriously."

The first vehicle to turn up was a pair of tandems, ridden in at speed by lycra-clad athletes.

Diana narrowed her eyes. "How is it possible to ride a bike without putting your feet down?"

Robin nodded. "We've seen bikes before. A regular bicycle won't work, but a tandem with someone else doing most of the work could. We'll see. It looks as though it's Errol and Ariadne. The two of them will have to sit on the back and resist any temptation to put their feet down. Tricky."

Diana could see Errol pointing to Ariadne and saying something to an assistant.

"Listen," said Robin. "I need to start recording a commentary. I can re-do it in the edit, but the spontaneous stuff is often what they like the best."

"I'll sit back and watch," said Diana.

Robin adopted the slightly frenzied speech patterns of racing commentators everywhere.

"It looks as though Errol and Ariadne will be first off the mark. It's a good job too, as Errol starts the race without the benefit of a win to give him that sixty second boost. They are trying a new approach to the bicycle idea, where they each sit on the rear of a tandem. This should overcome the difficulty of putting their feet down."

She peered at the screen, then made a low noise in her throat.

"Right, well I think we're seeing the first hint of acrimony on a team. Errol has asked for Ariadne's feet to be duct-taped to the pedals and she is *not* happy about it. Are we seeing some cracks in the teamwork here? Over the years, ego has been one of the largest impediments to success in this race. What will Errol do to address this? Now team Kamran have taken delivery of something on a covered trailer. Oh, it's a sedan chair! Sedan chairs come up a lot in the form of jokes, but I believe this is the first time we've seen a serious entry. It is of course intended to permit the party to use pavements if the roads are too congested."

Diana watched Robin zoom in on the apparatus.

"This sedan chair appears to be custom built. I believe that the construction is carbon fibre, and it consists of a chassis only. There are seats, but no roof, presumably to save weight. Is this the world's first racing sedan chair? Perhaps it's something we'll see more of, who knows?"

Diana was enjoying the commentary. She watched as Kamran and Zaf clambered on board the sedan chair and fastened themselves into bucket seats, facing each other.

"Here's our third conveyance," said Robin into the microphone. "Oxnard, always drawn to a retro aesthetic, has gone for something new. A vintage hearse, with a coffin in the back."

She zoomed in.

"Yes, it's a vintage Rolls-Royce, not sure of the model, but it's a beauty. Does Oxnard plan to fake a funeral procession? I believe he does."

Diana edged forward to see where Oxnard and Alexsei would sit. Was there room in the front? The rear door was opened by an undertaker and Diana clapped a hand over her mouth. Surely Oxnard wasn't about to put Alexsei in the coffin?

Alexsei's body language was casual. He climbed into the

rear of the hearse and disappeared head-first into the end of the coffin. Was Zaf watching? Probably not, as his sedan chair was currently being hefted up by a team of bulky men, facing away from the hearse.

"Well this is really quite novel," said Robin, "and especially intriguing because one of the passengers appears to be travelling inside the coffin, or coffin-like space. Oxnard himself is travelling in the front cab, beside the driver. Arguably there would have been room for Alexsei in the front too, but they might have fallen foul of seatbelt legislation."

Diana's attention was drawn to Alexsei's bodycam feed. She'd expected it to turn black inside the coffin, but instead it revealed a snug space in which it looked as if he was sitting in a chair, with drinks and snacks within reach.

Robin had noticed it too.

"Well it seems as though the coffin sits above a slightly larger space where Alexsei is actually quite comfortable. The hearse has now pulled away and is heading onto York Road where traffic is making way for it. Now we can see the true genius of this idea. The hearse is making excellent progress already. It's drawing some attention, though. I can see that the tandems of Team Errol have now started, and are attempting to ride in the slipstream of the hearse. Now I can see the sedan chair of Team Kamran heading out. I expect they will be planning to take the footbridge over the river, so they're heading in a different direction. The team doing the carrying look as if they've trained hard. They are moving at a good pace, and they've already shown that they can manoeuvre well in a tight spot."

Robin pulled up a map and focused in on the route.

"Team Kamran will have the edge if there are traffic holdups. If the hearse is able to clear a path using the power of politeness, then picking up speed will be possible, and that could give the advantage to both Team Oxnard and Team Errol."

Diana's phone finally connected.

"DCI Clint Sugarbrook," said the police detective.

Diana stood and moved away from Robin's control desk. "Detective, it's Diana Bakewell."

"Good," he replied. There was a lot of background noise. "I just thought I should give you a call."

"Your message sounded urgent."

"You read a lot into a very short text, Miss Bakewell."

"It's not urgent?"

"I just thought it was polite to let you know we found your man."

"My man?" she said, then understood. "You have found Vernon Monroth?"

"Yes. A body has washed up on the foreshore at Wapping."

CHAPTER FIFTY

"The man washed up almost directly on the Marine Policing Unit's doorstep," Sugarbrook continued. "We've not done a formal identification yet but he's got Monroth's wallet in his coat pocket."

There was a part of Diana that wanted to gloat, a part of her that wanted an immediate apology from each and every person who had doubted her, but she recognised that would be churlish in the extreme.

"I'm glad," she said. "I mean, I'm glad he's been found."

"We'd like to talk to you about it," said Sugarbrook. "I've got some questions I need to ask."

"Shall I come to you now?"

There was a pause.

"Give us an hour or two. If you could come over to Wapping... I'd say come to the Marine Policing Unit, but I don't fancy sharing an office with a huge pile of life vests and boating gear."

"The Town of Ramsgate pub is just down the road from the police station," Diana suggested.

Sugarbrook chuckled. "Do you know every back alley and drinking hole in London, Miss Bakewell?"

"I don't know. You'll have to test me."

"The Town of Ramsgate in two hours, then."

A thought occurred to her. "What's your opinion on dogs?"

"Dogs?"

"I've got a friend for you to meet."

Diana ended the call and returned to Robin's commentary on the race.

The live footage from the bodycams filled a row of monitors, and another showed the participants as moving dots on an illuminated map. Robin had dropped fully into the role of TV sports commentator, all for the benefit of the recorded highlights.

"Well this is quite extraordinary! Team Kamran, in the sedan chair, are not crossing the river using the footbridge but have in fact gone to the pier and are boarding a boat. This is permitted because the passengers have remained seated on the sedan chair. The boat looks to be vintage, although we'll have to check that. On a boat, the river will give them a clear run over a good part of the distance they need to cover, as well as providing much-needed rest for the chair-bearers."

The bodycams showed Kamran and Zaf's expressions. Kamran looked pleased with himself. Zaf looked exhilarated.

Diana turned to the dots on the tracker. Team Kamran's dots were moving more quickly than any of the others, speeding up the river unimpeded.

"The hearse of Team Oxnard has met with traffic problems around Parliament Square," said Robin. "That advantage of other road users giving way is less effective against very heavy traffic, and they've got no choice but to wait in line. Team Errol's tandems are taking advantage of their slimmer profile to dodge around the edges of the queue. I can't be certain, but I think that Errol's helper, Ariadne is in some distress."

Diana looked up. "What's happening?"

Robin zoomed in. "I think she's got some part of her clothing caught in the chain of the bike. It might be the hem of her trousers."

Robin's hand hovered over a large red button. She caught Diana's eye. "I can halt Errol if I think someone's in trouble. I'm not sure we're there yet, but I'm ready."

They both stared at the screen.

Robin's commentary continued. "The progress of their tandem has stalled because of the entanglement. Wait! I can see that another cyclist is approaching them. I think it's someone from Errol's support team. He's grabbed Ariadne's trouser leg and has taken some sort of a blade to it. The tandem is back on the road now, but Team Errol has lost that slight lead and is now neck-and-neck with the hearse of Team Oxnard as they emerge from the worst of the traffic into Knightsbridge."

Diana couldn't remember Ariadne's trousers being especially wide-legged. It would be annoying to have them spoiled in that way.

"And let's get back to Team Kamran on their boat," Robin continued. "They have pulled up at a rowing club and are being carried onto the pontoon. The crew carrying that chair are certainly earning their money today. After a brief rest on the river, they must now take the weight of Kamran and Zaf and make the final dash to Hammersmith tube station."

The map showed how far ahead Kamran and Zaf were. The others stood no chance of catching up now.

"Something's happening with Team Errol!" shouted Robin. "This is, um... I don't even know what it is yet."

The feed was confusing. The support rider was beside

Ariadne, fastening her into some sort of harness. He then bent down to cut away the duct tape at her feet. Errol was also in a harness. As Diana watched, they were borne upwards and away, leaving the tandems below them.

"They are being suspended from drones," said Robin, her mouth falling open. "Errol and Ariadne are being carried through the air by drones. This changes everything."

Diana watched the dots converge around Hammersmith station. Robin switched to another view, a camera positioned at the destination.

"We will record them coming in. We might need those timestamps if it's a close finish."

Diana leaned in close to Robin, watching the final moments tick away. Zaf and Kamran were being carried at a trot through side roads and across the busy junction on the final approach to Hammersmith station. Errol and Ariadne could be seen floating through the air. There was an appalled grimace on Ariadne's face, and even Errol looked unsettled.

"I think Team Errol have been grazing the tops of the trees," said Robin, "based on the greenery attached to their clothes."

"It's going to be close!" said Diana.

The two teams were both in view of the camera at the station, although coming in at very different angles. The sedan chair romped along the pavement, people swerving out of its way as it approached. The drones plummeted from the sky in a manner that must have been quite unnerving, and people on the pavement were clearly alarmed.

"Yesss!" screamed Errol as he touched down ahead of Kamran. He did a victory dance, yanking off the drone harness with irritation. Ariadne touched down and scrambled to remove her harness. She looked like someone who wanted to sit down quietly, possibly with a stiff drink.

Kamran and Zaf arrived on their sedan chair and stepped off as it was lowered to the ground.

It was another four minutes before Oxnard pulled up in his hearse.

"And that marks the end of the race," said Robin. "Everyone will return to the control room where I will declare the winner."

"Exciting stuff," said Diana. She looked at her watch and mentally calculated the time it would take her to get to Wapping. "I'd best go."

"Places to be?" said Robin.

"Got to see a man about a dog," she said and left to collect Turner from the depot.

CHAPTER FIFTY-ONE

Z<small>AF</small> <small>DIDN'T FEEL</small> he'd helped all that much in the race. The four men who'd carried him and Kamran across London insisted it was what they'd trained for, but he couldn't help regretting the extra sausage at breakfast, adding to their load.

He sat with a grin plastered across his face as they drove along the north bank of the Thames in yet another limo. Kamran pointed things out along the way, but Zaf was oblivious. It seemed to be property that he owned, or was thinking of buying, or that one of the others owned.

"So, d'you think you've won?" Zaf asked.

Kamran held up a hand. "I make no assumptions. Robin's word is final, and she may apply penalties, who knows? This competition is important, but I have learned that it's important to not leap ahead." He leaned back. "So let's enjoy the ride."

Zaf wasn't sure if he was supposed to be enjoying the metaphorical ride or the actual one, but it probably didn't matter. This would be his last time in Kamran's fancy limo, so he leaned back and luxuriated in the leather seats and the plush floor, stretching out his legs.

Alexsei was waiting for them at the rooftop bar of the spa. He kissed Zaf.

"A fun day, no?" he said.

"I think I had a better day than Ariadne, by the look on her face."

"I imagine she might benefit from a drink."

Zaf stroked his boyfriend's arm, his gaze not leaving his face. "My thoughts exactly."

Alexsei smiled into Zaf's eyes. "Drinks all round."

"Definitely." Zaf's phone was ringing. "It's Newton. I'd better talk to him, in case he's been arrested again."

He stepped away to take the call.

"Zaf!" said Newton. "I've had a brilliant idea."

"Brilliant idea?"

"About the shoes. Come downstairs."

"Downstairs where?"

"Outside the spa reception. You *are* here, aren't you?"

Zaf shrugged at Alexsei then hurried down to reception, which was quite crowded. Newton stood outside in his overalls.

He pulled Zaf to one side. "I need to get inside to do some work. It's not going to take more than half an hour, but I need access."

"What is it?"

"Best you don't know, in case anyone asks. I'm sure you'll approve, though."

"Fine," said Zaf. "It's a good time to come in now. It's really busy."

Zaf picked up the toolbox at Newton's side, while Newton wrestled a large box through the door. They engaged in intense chatter as they passed through reception, avoiding eye contact with any of the other groups.

As they approached the stairs, Newton spotted a doorway and opened it to reveal a large store cupboard. "This will do me nicely to put some bits and bobs together. See you later."

"What?" said Zaf.

"Leave me to it. This is definitely going to work."

Zaf wasn't so sure. But leaving Newton to whatever he was up to would probably be best for all concerned.

CHAPTER FIFTY-TWO

The Town of Ramsgate pub sat on Wapping High Street, a pleasantly quiet street bordered by old warehouses on one side, waterfront buildings and the river itself on the other. The pub was a listed building with wooden panelling and inscribed glass, as well as a convivial atmosphere.

With Turner by her side, Diana went inside and found DCI Clint Sugarbrook sitting at the far end near the rear door. Detective Sergeant Quigley was with him.

Diana ordered a tonic water and refills of whatever the police detectives were having, then went to sit with them. Turner hopped up onto the fourth seat at the table as if he was about to join in the conversation. Diana stroked his head automatically as he sat.

"We appreciate you coming to speak to us," said Sugarbrook.

"Despite not following up when I told the police what I saw."

"That's not entirely fair. We simply didn't have enough to go on." He closed his eyes momentarily. "If you feel you've been let down, then we apologise. And we are grateful you have come to see us."

"You found Monroth, then?" she asked.

Sugarbrook looked out of the back door. There was a rear terrace backing onto the water.

"About fifty feet downstream from this very spot," he said. "The Marine Policing Unit think he must have got caught on something upstream for a day or so before working loose. Yes. We have him."

Diana pointed at Turner. "This is his dog."

Sugarbrook frowned. "What do you mean?"

"This is Turner. Named after the famous painter. He was on Vernon Monroth's boat when I paid a visit yesterday and—"

"You went to his houseboat?"

"No one else seemed to care one fig for this man, Detective Chief Inspector. Yes, I went to his houseboat. And somehow acquired a dog in the process."

"Where is this boat?"

"Gallions Point. Near City Airport."

Sugarbrook looked at DS Quigley. She nodded, stood and made her way out, pulling out her phone as she moved.

The DCI sighed. "Diana Bakewell. Sticking her nose in again when it's not wanted."

"I've been roundly ignored by the police, while trying to draw their attention to this man's death."

"Yes, yes," he replied wearily. "Point taken."

"But you've asked me here for a reason. I'm not just here to receive an apology."

He nodded. "I need to ask what you saw on the day Vernon Monroth died. There are some unexplained aspects of the case. This Vernon Monroth is not unknown to the police."

"I gather he was a dodgy character."

"What do you gather?"

Diana leaned back in her seat. "He was once a very successful art dealer. He knew and worked with a man called Oxnard Pike, one of our clients this week. Pike is the owner of the yacht that Vernon fell from."

"You do mingle with members of high society, don't you?"

"Zaf and I have been involved in some rich men's games. Oxnard Pike, Errol van Blerk and Kamran Dadashov, playing extravagant and childish games in memory of their friend, Tristram Ramsgate."

"I've read that name," said Sugarbrook. He looked under the trench coat folded on the seat next to him and pulled out a manila folder. "It's in here..."

As he searched, the barmaid passed them with two plates of food. Turner's head followed the smell while Diana held onto his collar and stroked him to keep him in place. Outside, the river glowed in the afternoon sun.

"They captured 'Hanging' Judge Jeffreys here, you know," she said.

"Pardon?" said Sugarbrook, skimming the notes.

"Hanging Judge Jeffreys. Sixteen hundreds. Sent a lot of innocent men to the gallows, often to curry favour with King James the Second and to support the Catholic-leaning monarchy. When the Glorious Revolution forced James to flee, Judge Jeffreys stayed in London a little longer than was good for him."

"Is that so?"

Diana sipped her drink. "I think he thought he had just been doing right by his employer, the king. But he was recognised in this pub, despite the fact that he'd shaved off his notable eyebrows, and the men who recognised him had been on the receiving end of his particular brand of justice and didn't have much sympathy for him."

"Ah!" said Sugarbrook, finding his page. "This is it. Court record. Vernon Monroth appeared as a witness at the inquest into Tristram Ramsgate's death."

"Did he?"

Witness to events at London Freeport development site on day of the accident, it says."

"Oh. That's interesting."

"Is it? You know about that?"

"The rough details," Diana replied. "Tristram Ramsgate had a built a freeport storage facility further out along the Thames. It's all a tax dodge as far as I can tell."

"A simplification, I'm sure."

"All of the men we've been working with were involved. Errol van Blerk's company was involved in construction. Kamran Dadashov's engineering people had installed the security and safety systems which ultimately killed Ramsgate."

"How?"

"Halon gas."

Sugarbrook sucked his teeth at the thought.

"Oxnard Pike was due to store artworks there," said Diana. "I guess Monroth might have been there to oversee their delivery or something."

"So, he was there when this Tristam fellow died."

"Possibly."

The postcards Monroth had received from his intended blackmail victim were in her bag. Sugarbrook should know Monroth was attempting blackmail. If someone had deliberately killed Monroth, then that was the obvious motive. *If* someone had murdered Monroth...

She knew what she'd seen. She'd seen Monroth go into the

covered lounge area on the yacht and come flying out again as though punched or thrown. And yet Oxnard, the obvious suspect, had been standing right beside her.

"The thing I needed to discuss with you," said Sugarbrook, "is the fact that Vernon Monroth had injuries on his body when he was pulled from the water."

"Oh?" said Diana.

"Unusual injuries."

CHAPTER FIFTY-THREE

"WHAT ARE THESE, THEN?" asked Alexsei, sitting down by Zaf in the rooftop seating.

A pair of tall colourful cocktails stood in front of them. Each had a sprig of celery sticking out of the top but Zaf wasn't sure of their true health value.

They were waiting for Errol van Blerk and Ariadne to return to the spa for the final adjudication. It appeared that the need for a stiff drink after the day's excitement had seized Ariadne, and she and Errol had taken themselves to a Hammersmith bar to recuperate. Zaf wondered if it was a bar Errol already owned, and if it wasn't, whether he'd offered to buy it yet.

He gestured at the open folders before him. "Diana left these with me. They belonged to the dead guy."

"The river guy?" said Alexsei.

He nodded. "Vernon Monroth. Dodgy art dealer. Your dad probably knew him back in the day."

Alexsei shook his head. "I do not know the name."

"Anyway, this is his scrapbook of artworks. Like this one,

this Renoir. We only know it exists in its entirety because it appears in this other bloke's painting."

"A painting within a painting. Two figures within a much larger scene."

"And all these others," said Zaf, flicking through. "They're all artworks that have, well, gone missing. No one knows where they are."

"Was this man trying to track them down? Was that his business strategy?"

Zaf tilted his head. "Finding missing or stolen artworks and then selling them on at a profit? Could be."

Alexsei picked up the other folder and looked through. "Seems a tough way to make a living."

Zaf searched on his phone for Vernon Monroth. The man hadn't had a significant online presence. His name was in no mainstream news articles. However, there were minor news pieces, archived items linked to the fine art industry. At least one looked interesting.

"Here," he said. "This article is nearly twenty years old but... portrait of Empress Elizabeth of Russia by Giovani Battista Tiepolo ... blah, blah, blah... found in an attic in Denmark... authenticated by some Dutch art institute with evidence provided by Vernon Monroth. Sold to a private collector in London."

"So that is how he made his money," said Alexsei.

"That London collector could have been Oxnard." Zaf sipped his drink, poking himself with the stick of celery. "Vernon Monroth was a crooked character."

"You know this?" said Alexsei.

"It's what Big Ernie told Diana. Apparently."

"Big Ernie is the uncle who owns a butcher's in the East

End, yes? The man who kindly provided all the meat for Diana's birthday barbecue?"

"Well, he's not actually her uncle. And he doesn't just own a butcher's. And he's kind but... but only if you stay on his right side. Apparently he duffed up one of Diana's real cousins the other night because of something the man shouldn't have said in a local pub. But, yes, him. And I trust him to spot a fellow crook when he sees one."

"Also Big Ernie is not so big, I think."

"Dieting, I hear."

"So Vernon Monroth is a corrupt individual. I mean, was."

Zaf put his drink down. "What kind of artwork does Oxnard Pike own? Have you seen his collection?"

Alexsei laughed. "No one gets to see Oxnard's art. He never loans it out. Never puts it on display. Owning it is the source of his wealth and I sometimes think the only pleasure he gets from it is owning something that no one else can see."

"What if...?" Zaf hesitated. He didn't want to blurt out wild speculations. "Has anyone ever considered the possibility that some of Oxnard's art, the stuff he owns... has anyone ever suggested that it just doesn't exist?"

"What do you mean?"

"There's art that people know exists but then goes missing," said Zaf, waving his hands over the folders. "And then it's found and... certain individuals, with information gained from the clever but crooked Vernon Monroth, they say it's the real deal and it gets sold for an undisclosed amount to Oxnard Pike."

"You say he owns fakes?"

"Maybe not even that. Maybe he owns bits of paper that say he owns valuable paintings. Because no one ever sees them, there doesn't even *need* to be a fake. He owns so much art, maybe no one has ever actually catalogued what he really has. I doubt he even knows himself every bit of art he owns."

"No." Alexsei screwed up his face in thought. "No. I don't think...." He hummed to himself. "No. That's too outlandish. I mean, why?"

"You could secure loans against them, for one thing," said Zaf. "Sell shares in them. It's like the gold in the Bank of England."

"Is it?"

Zaf looked in his wallet for a bank note and was surprised to find one. "Look here. *I promise to pay the bearer on demand the sum of.* That used to be a real and true promise that you could go and get your five or ten quid's worth of gold from the Bank of England. Bank notes were just that, promises that you could have the gold."

"There's no gold in the Bank of England now?"

"Actually," said Zaf, "there's something like forty thousand bars of the stuff. But the bank only actually owns two of them. Point is, there's not physical gold that your bank note can be swapped for. But the economy still works."

"And you think Oxnard's personal business might work the same way?"

Zaf waved his hand. "Idle speculation. But it explains these folders of art research Monroth had."

His phone rang: Newton. He picked up.

"How goes the secret project, Newton?"

"My masterpiece is complete," replied Newton. "You should come down and see it."

"OK." Zaf looked at Alexsei. "Want to come see Newton's masterpiece?"

"More art?"

"I've got no idea."

CHAPTER FIFTY-FOUR

"THE MARINE POLICING lads made it very clear that a body is unlikely to spend three days in the Thames without picking up injuries," Sugarbrook explained to Diana in the Town of Ramsgate pub. "They get bashed about by bridge struts or passing boats or what have you."

"I see," she said.

"But this injury is perplexing." Sugarbrook held up his hands, fingers splayed. "Did you see any injuries on Vernon Monroth's hand when you saw him, alive, near the London Eye?"

"Injuries?" She paused in her stroking of Turner. The little dog licked her hand to remind her of his existence, and she went back to patting his head. "No. I don't recall any."

"Burn injuries."

"Burns?"

Sugarbrook indicated on his raised hand. "Burns along all the fingers of his right hand."

Diana tried to picture what she recalled of the man when he'd collided with her.

"No. No, I don't think so."

"The pathologist's initial thoughts are that they occurred very close to his time of death. He'd either gripped something very hot or received burns through some other method, electric shock or chemicals or similar."

"I don't remember seeing anything," she said. "Sorry."

"That's fine. The autopsy might provide us with clearer details."

"Will it help you understand why he died or who killed him?"

"At this point, he might just be a man who slipped overboard from a yacht and accidentally drowned. It does happen."

Diana couldn't put it off any longer. She delved into her handbag and pulled out the postcards.

"These were on Vernon Monroth's houseboat," she said, passing them over.

Sugarbrook was agog.

"Diana! You've been stealing evidence?"

"Not exactly."

"Then *what* exactly?" he demanded, his voice rising in a way that made the man at the next table turn and look. "I take it you went inside to get these. You didn't find them outside the houseboat?"

"Well, no—"

"Then that's breaking and entering, at least. Theft for certain. I should arrest you right now."

She pulled her back straight. "I was trying to do right by the man, when the police weren't interested."

"You were sticking your nose in as always," he growled. "I don't know who you think you are, Diana Bakewell. Your intimate knowledge of every bit of London – bent judges hanging people to appease their masters or whatever – it just makes you come across as smug and self-satisfied. The fact that you act like everyone in London is your best mate. You probably know the name of that barmaid there."

"Tanya? Yes, I—"

"You swan about like you own this city. No, you glide above it. Here, there and everywhere, like Mary bleeding Poppins. It doesn't make you better than the rest of us. It doesn't give you the right to interfere with things that are none of your business. You are an insufferable, interfering woman who needs to get a proper hobby."

A knot of anger had grown in Diana's stomach. He wasn't going to intimidate her.

"Have you quite finished, Detective?" she asked, her voice level.

"I bloody well haven't. I've half a mind to put you in handcuffs now."

She raised an eyebrow. "See how that looks, putting a sweet old lady—"

"Ha! Don't you play the sweet old lady card with me, Diana. You are none of those things."

"Maybe I am not. But I tell you what I am. I'm caring. I actually care."

"The London Metropolitan Police cares about—"

"No," she said. "You do what you have to, when you have to. I mean *care*. I was the only one that saw Vernon Monroth had died. I was the only one who seemed to care that he had ever lived. He might have been a scoundrel, maybe an art fraudster, maybe a thief. Maybe he even killed Tristram Ramsgate. I don't know. But he was a human being and I seemed to be the only one who cared! And when I went to his houseboat and saw a little dog on board, locked inside, I was the only one who cared enough to let him out. How could I resist a cute dog like that?"

She paused in the acting of patting the dog's head and stared.

"Oh, hell," she whispered, her throat suddenly dry.

"What is it?" said Sugarbrook. "Are you alright?"

"I..." Diana stared at the dog. She took a sip of her drink. "Oh, my goodness."

"What?" demanded Sugarbrook, his tone more concerned.

She looked at him. "I know how he died."

"Monroth?"

"Yes. I know."

"He drowned," said Sugarbrook. "I don't think that's in doubt."

"No. Not necessarily. I know how he was killed. And I know how Oxnard didn't need to be there to do it."

"What? You think Oxnard Pike killed him."

She stared at her hand. "Yes. Possibly. I think I can see how it was done and, oh, it's fiendish."

She stood, full of energy. "I need to check something."

"You're not leaving my sight," said Sugarbrook.

"This might not be exactly legal. It's... definitely not legal."

"Then you're *definitely* not going."

"Please." She passed Turner's string lead to Sugarbrook. "I need you to look after Turner. He's no bother at all."

She was halfway to the door when Sugarbrook called out to her.

"Where are you going?"

"I'm going to find the murder weapon."

CHAPTER FIFTY-FIVE

Together, Zaf and Alexsei walked down to the reception of the Serenity Haven spa.

Zaf was surprised to find a crowd of well-dressed women clustered around what could only be described as a new installation. He edged forward to see what had captured their interest.

A large white shelving unit was flush against the wall. It was one of those units that formed a lattice shape to display a collection. In this case, the collection consisted of a number of individual women's shoes.

Above the unit was a small, handwritten caption.

Shoe Me The Way to Go. This temporary artwork celebrates the urban artistry of the designer shoe. Browse the exquisite craftsmanship and feel the power of the women who wear these.

Recognise your shoe? If you leave it for the full length of the exhibition then you will be rewarded for your patronage of the arts with a magnum of Champagne. See reception. Please add your name to the list of patrons on the side, and Thank You.

Zaf recognised Newton's neat handwriting. He looked around to see how people were reacting.

"It's an under-recognised artform," said one woman. "I love it."

"I'm all in favour of guerilla art, but I wish they'd asked," said another. "Those Jimmy Choos are my favourites. I wanted to wear them tomorrow."

"Oh pish. You'll just have to buy some more, won't you? You can't destroy art."

"No. I suppose I can't." The woman retrieved a pen from her Birkin bag and added her name to the list on the wall. "I suppose someone has called the papers? This could be bigger than Banksy!"

Zaf caught a glimpse of Newton on the pavement outside and wandered out to meet him.

"This?" said Zaf, with a thumb over his shoulder at the art installation. "This was your brilliant idea?"

"I'm really pleased with it," said Newton with an impish grin.

"But it's mad."

Newton gave a shrug. "They get their shoes back, after a fashion. I get rid of the shoes from the depot, which is an absolute weight off my mind, I can tell you. And if Gus decides to steal any more, then we have a mechanism for returning them to their owners."

"But..."

"But what?"

"How can anyone just put some shoes on display and declare it to be art?"

"Art can be anything you want it to be, and it can serve a multitude of purposes," declared Newton.

His chest swelled. He was the picture of a man both

pleased and at peace with himself. He turned towards the depot and met Gus sauntering across the road towards the spa.

"Ah, ah, ah," said Newton firmly. "Not today, mister! Back you go. Let's leave the ladies in peace with their shoes." He scooped the cat up in his arms and carried him away.

Shaking his head, Zaf made to go back inside. His phone was ringing again, Diana this time. He picked up.

"Tell me," said Diana, her voice a low whisper. "What do you know about art?"

"Funny you should say that," said Zaf. "It seems I know absolutely nothing."

"Well, I might need your help."

"Where are you?"

"I'm about to sneak back onto Oxnard's yacht."

"Why?"

"I need to see about a dog."

"I thought you'd already gone to see a man about a dog."

"Different dog," she said. "If I'm right, this one's bite is worse than its bark."

CHAPTER FIFTY-SIX

For the second time in a week, Diana descended the steps by the embankment wall and made her way onto the pier. The *Silver Salmon*, with its three decks rising above the waterline, the Starchaser manufacturer logo on the side, stood out as a floating mansion among the other yachts.

She strolled to the gangplank, swinging her arms. She stepped onto the rear deck, once again devoid of visible crew.

"So," she muttered into her phone, "I'm thinking that Vernon was killed on the yacht."

"Right," said Zaf. "We know that."

"I mean that he might have been dead before he hit the water."

She stepped into the yacht's lounge. As before, there was a mixture of luxurious if uninspiring furnishings and walls crowded with art.

"I'm going to send you a photo," she said, "and I want you to tell me if you know anything about it or can find out about it."

"OK."

She held her phone out and pointed it at the stainless-steel dog statue in the middle of the floor beside the rough bronze. The dog was a little larger than life-size and of a simple design, but its attentive posture gave it character. She sent it over to Zaf.

A moment later, Zaf said, "It's a dog."

"I was hoping for a little more than that."

"It's a very nice dog," added Alexsei's voice in the background.

Diana approached the dog. "If you don't hear from me in the next sixty seconds, call an ambulance and send them to the *Silver Salmon*."

"What?"

Sixty seconds. No more. *Silver Salmon*."

"Blimey, Diana. What are you up to?"

Diana stood in front of the dog so she could see her own reflection in it. She reached out and carefully tapped its forehead with her brolly. The statue made a 'ting' sound but nothing more. Moving very carefully, she then placed a fingertip on the dog's head. It was cool to the touch. She adjusted her hand and put her whole palm on its head, as though patting it. Nothing unusual occurred.

"Of course," she whispered. "I patted him last time."

She could hear Zaf's voice from her phone, but she wasn't finished yet.

She dipped into her handbag until she found the metallic remote button thing she'd picked up at the dinner table on Wednesday evening. She stepped back and pressed the button. A slight, almost inaudible humming sound started up from the steel dog.

"Bloody hell." She took another step back. She pressed the button again and the humming stopped.

Zaf was now shouting from her phone. She put it to her ear. "Yes, yes. I'm all fine. Not dead at all. You can stop panicking."

"I've got no idea what you're up to, Diana, but please don't make me worry like that."

"Apologies, Zaf. Any info on the dog statue?"

"Still searching."

She nodded. "I'll get off. Message me if you find anything."

The dog device was turned off again and she placed her hand on it once more. Imagining she was Monroth, she gave a slight convulsion and pretended to stagger back from the dog. It was only three or four steps from here – possibly fewer, for a man – out through the open rear of the lounge area to the edge of the deck.

"Zap, step, step, splash," she said.

She turned at the sound of footsteps in the inner section of the yacht. The captain in his silly uniform came through a small door, another crew member in tow.

"Excuse me... you! What are you doing here?"

"Ah, Captain," she said. "I came back with further questions."

He waved a hand. "I've got no time for this." He turned to his companion. "Radio the police. Tell them we've caught someone breaking in."

CHAPTER FIFTY-SEVEN

A REVERSE IMAGE search on the internet had brought up some possible answers to the mystery of the dog statue. Zaf and Alexsei looked over the results together.

"There's an artist in Toledo who does moulded steel animals," said Zaf.

"Or there's this one in Berkshire," suggested Alexsei. "Just outside London."

"None of them seem to have constructed a dog quite like this one."

"I think the style is more like the British one than the Spanish one."

Zaf nodded. "And if Oxnard's got one on his yacht, it'd make sense to get it from the British artist."

"Is everything alright?" asked Robin, entering the roof garden.

Zaf whirled, surprised by the feeling of guilt at being caught in the act of investigative research.

"Um, yes. Yes, of course."

"Good," said Robin. "Errol and Ariadne have returned. It is time for the final adjudication."

"We're ready," said Zaf. "Absolutely."

"Good. I'm sure it will be a dramatic climax," she said. "High stakes stuff, you understand."

Alexsei laughed. "Who will get to put Tristram's ashes on their mantelpiece this year?"

"Things are as important as we make them," said Robin. She turned and went downstairs.

Zaf and Alexsei followed and were soon seated in the dining room, with Robin's screens now set up behind her. A couple of open bottles of wine were on the table and it was clear that Errol van Blerk and Ariadne Webb had been helping themselves.

"Zaf and Alexsei have now joined us," said Robin.

"No Diana this time?" asked Kamran.

"Might be joining us in a bit," said Zaf.

"I think we're all assembled, so I can begin," said Robin. "Now I think you've all had a good race. There were some interesting choices made with the conveyances this year. We'll talk about each one in turn, shall we? In the meantime, I've taken some stats from your tracker apps, with average speeds, ascents, descents and in some cases, altitudes."

Robin showed a screen filled with graphs and statistics. Zaf gave it a quick glance, but was more interested in the commentary.

"I will approach this in reverse order of finishing time," said Robin. "So we will begin with Oxnard and Alexsei, who arrived in third place. Team Oxnard had a sixty-second advantage for winning the Egg Sandwich Challenge." A leaderboard appeared, displaying Oxnard's finish time. The numbers whirred and a minute was removed. "Now, what about penalties? Oxnard stuck with the same method of conveyance throughout, a beautiful Rolls Royce hearse, modified so that Alexsei didn't have to actually lie in a coffin. That's good, because I might have applied a penalty for that."

Oxnard gave a small nod.

"The vintage nature of the hearse means that it's permitted within the rules. The social effect of seeing a hearse removed obstacles in a most ingenious way, and I can't apply an inconvenience penalty because people chose to let you pass. So in summary, no time penalties apply to Oxnard."

There was a round of applause.

"Next, we come to Kamran and Zaf, who arrived in second place. We all know that pedestrian options can work well over shorter distances or in the case of congestion. The sedan chair took advantage of that effect, and it was fascinating to see your design."

"I bought a company that manufactures racing jet skis," said Kamran, his eyes sparkling. "They made this for me."

"Nice. You got off to a swift start, then moved to the water. There is no doubt that river transport was a good option, and the sedan chair made sure that your feet didn't touch the ground. Your team were able to take a quick breather before they had to bear you on to the final destination. I was impressed by their strength and stamina, by the way. So the strategy was well thought out. A rapid start and a river crew on standby helped you to create a fast combination. But... there is a small problem with the craft you used."

Kamran raised his eyebrows in surprise.

"The craft itself is from the nineteen twenties, a classic motor launch, and that is permitted. What you perhaps didn't know is that it had a reconditioned engine fitted six years ago.

That was manufactured in the nineteen eighties, and is therefore too new. A two-minute penalty applies."

"Ugh!" Kamran growled and rolled his eyes, but he didn't argue.

"Finally, we move on to Errol, who arrived first. Now this was a well thought out combination of transport methods. Tandems overcome the problem we've seen before with bicycles, where it is inevitable that the rider's feet will contact the road. And drones are not something we've seen before. It added a new dimension which we will need to talk about. First and foremost though, the most pressing point I want to address is the comfort and safety of Ariadne, which was, I think, neglected somewhat."

Ariadne looked stricken. "I was perfectly fine!" Her voice wobbled from one too many recuperative drinks.

"You were not fine. You were fastened to a bicycle which tore your unsuitable clothing. You were then hoisted into the air on a drone, and I don't believe you were briefed on any of these beforehand, nor were you able to give your consent to being physically constrained."

"I have papers!" said Errol. "She signed them at the beginning."

Robin ignored him. "A five minute-penalty is applied. Now let's move on to the matter of the drone. We have a rule regarding vehicles with internal combustion engines, which must predate nineteen seventy. This rule is in urgent need of updating, because it overlooks any vehicles powered by electric motors. In theory, you could all drive electric cars, but it would be against the spirit of that rule, and I think you're all aware of that. In the same way, the use of drones is also against the spirit of that rule. And so I am applying a sixty second penalty and updating the rules for next year."

Errol made a sound like a punctured balloon. "Eish! That is very severe!"

The numbers on the leaderboard rattled and whirred for dramatic effect and then resolved to final timings.

"Here you can see the final, adjusted scores. Kamran, with an adjusted time of thirty-four minutes, is our winner and the recipient of the ashes trophy. Well done Kamran and Zaf!"

Kamran stood and pulled Zaf in for a huge bear hug, squeezing the air from his lungs. "Good teamwork!" he cried, then turned to shake hands with Oxnard and Errol.

While everyone shook hands and bellowed their reactions across the room, there came a knock at the door. Mindy from reception entered, followed by Diana and the broad-shouldered figure of DCI Sugarbrook along with the much smaller detective sergeant, Quigley.

"More people come to celebrate?" asked Errol.

"Sorry to interrupt your gathering, everyone," said Sugarbrook. "I'm Detective Chief Inspector Clint Sugarbrook. I wonder if I could speak to you all for a moment."

"Oh, dear," chortled Errol. "I think someone here has been violating English traffic laws."

Zaf looked at Diana, but her face was giving nothing away. Was this about Vernon Monroth?

"I'm afraid it's much more serious than that, sir." Sugarbrook withdrew a plastic bag from his pocket. It contained what looked like a small remote-control device. "I need to ask some questions about the murder of Mr Vernon Monroth."

CHAPTER FIFTY-EIGHT

"Vᴇʀɴᴏɴ Mᴏɴʀᴏᴛʜ?" said Errol. "I haven't heard that name in years."

"You know the man, do you, sir?" said Sugarbrook.

"We don't know anything about any murder," said Kamran.

Sugarbrook tilted his head towards Diana. "Miss Bakewell here has a story to tell, and I for one find it somewhat compelling."

"Really?" huffed Oxnard. "We have places to be, things to do, and if you want to waste my time, Mr Policeman, then I think you'll need to hear from my legal team first."

Diana looked straight at Oxnard.

"Mr Pike. I know you killed Vernon Monroth. I'm fairly certain I know how and I think... I think... I know why."

Zaf frowned. He and Diana had been discussing Vernon's death, and the possible explanations for it, for much of the week. But she hadn't claimed to understand it all.

"Is this a piece of avant-garde theatre or something?" asked Errol.

"Oh, I do hope so," said Ariadne with a grin.

"I'm afraid it isn't," said Sugarbrook, pulling out his ID. "I'm a very real police officer."

"It's all to do with Tristram Ramsgate's death," said Diana, stepping to the foot of the long table. "He died quite a few years ago, but conversations this week have allowed all of us an insight into how that happened. It was during the final stages of the construction of the freeport storage facility further down the Thames. And, at times, you have all held each other accountable for his death."

Kamran's face was hard. "We have come together this week to mourn him and celebrate him. Not to rake over the ashes of a tragedy."

Diana looked at him. "He was asphyxiated in one of the storage areas by the fire suppression system. It was a Dadashov system that controlled the security and the fire safety systems. And the whole project was constructed by Mr van Blerk's construction company."

"If you're about to sling accusations around, girl," said van Blerk, "then you are entering a world of legal pain."

She cocked her head. Zaf felt Alexsei move closer to him. He wanted to grasp his boyfriend's hand. Did Alexsei know anything about his father's involvement in this?

"You yourself happily told me that your company favours working quickly over all other considerations," Diana said to van Blerk. "That you *sail close to the wind* frequently. Your own friends here said that you squeeze suppliers to get the lowest possible costs."

"I will take slander like that to court. You'll be sued for everything you own."

"I can assure you, that won't take long, Errol," she replied. "I own very little. Meanwhile, you'll all recall that Mr Pike's insistence that the project be finished quickly so his precious art collection could be stored there has been cited by people at this table as a contributing factor to Mr Ramsgate's death."

"I will not stand for any more of this nonsense," said Oxnard.

DCI Sugarbrook had his eye on Pike, Zaf realised. He was waiting to see what Diana had to say, just like the rest of them. But he was also ready to act.

"Your collection of art lies at the centre of all this," Diana said to Oxnard.

"How so?"

"I suspect that much, perhaps most, perhaps nearly all of it does not exist."

"Gibberish nonsense," spat Pike.

"The dead man, whose body the police have now recovered, is one Vernon Monroth. I think most of you have heard of him, if you haven't met him. Mr Pike knows him, although he was hesitant to admit as much when I mentioned it. Mr Monroth was a crooked art dealer. He seemed to specialise in falsifying what was required to give authentication to paintings of dubious provenance. He had several folders of artworks that are lost to the art world but which I suspect he was very happy to magically 'find' and then declare to be the genuine article."

"You have proof of this?" asked Robin.

"A lot of circumstantial details," Diana replied. "This week I've had it demonstrated to me time and again that things, real or otherwise, have as much value as people are willing to ascribe to them. Whether that's the ancient ice in our drinks here or over-priced designer shoes or the stone coins of the Yap islanders."

"Yap islanders?" said Alexsei.

"Another time," said Diana. "The point is, things have value because we say they do."

Zaf, thinking about what he'd told Alexsei about the money in the Bank of England, nodded.

"One set of tickets from the London Eye gets us on the ride," said Diana. "Another set is refused at the barrier. Real or fake? It's all down to a consensus on what the world will accept. And Vernon Monroth excelled at blurring that line. And – I think – that's why he killed Tristram Ramsgate."

"I beg your pardon?" said Robin.

"Speculation on my part," said Diana, "but he was at the facility on the day of Tristram's death. He was a witness at the inquest, after all. And I'm wondering if something in the conversation between them that day, or perhaps something Tristram saw, revealed that the art Oxnard insisted on storing there was, well, nothing but blank canvasses and empty storage boxes."

"Wait," said Zaf. "Why would someone store art that doesn't exist? That's crazy."

"How better to ensure the world continues to accept the authenticity of a hidden artwork than by hiding it in an expensive and exclusive storage facility? Putting your imaginary treasures in a big solid box would only cement their existence and their value. And what if, in that moment of unfortunate discovery at the freeport storage facility, Vernon Monroth activated a fire alarm and," she shrugged, "perhaps pushed Tristram into a room as the security measures took over? Or what if he simply failed to help Tristram out? I don't know."

"Doesn't know!" Oxnard snarled. "Speculation! Theories! I'm calling a stop to this now."

"Oxnard," said Errol, in a firmer voice than Zaf had heard him use before. "I am keen to hear this woman out."

"What?"

"If there's any truth in this..." agreed Kamran, his voice lower.

Diana nodded her thanks.

"Vernon would have been driven by greed, or a weird sort of loyalty. I happened to be at the pub where Hanging Judge Jeffreys was arrested earlier today. He sent hundreds to their deaths, often because it was what he thought the king wanted. And he assumed that he would have the king's protection when he did so."

She reached for her handbag then stopped, frowning.

"I had some postcards, now in police evidence. Sent to Vernon, referring to certain 'demands' Vernon had made of the sender. *You have as much to lose as me* and other such phrases. They directly reference the death that both Vernon and his blackmail target were responsible for."

She paused, her gaze roaming the room. Zaf put out a hand and felt it brush against Alexsei's.

"One of the postcards invited Vernon to meet with the unnamed sender," Diana continued.

She focused on Oxnard.

"You, Mr Pike."

CHAPTER FIFTY-NINE

"THE POSTCARDS WERE of a distinctive vintage design," said Diana. "All of them. And the shop they came from sold a batch to you, Mr Pike. Delivered to your house. It's there in the ledger."

"You're spouting drivel," exclaimed Oxnard. "I don't even know what you're talking about."

"And," she continued, "the postcard requesting a meeting is what led Vernon to come to your yacht on Tuesday while we were on the London Eye."

"You invited him there?" Kamran said to Oxnard.

"There's a brilliant recklessness to the idea," said Diana. "Years after Tristram's death, Vernon came to you wanting a pay-off of some sort for keeping quiet about the whole thing. And so you invited him to come and speak to you at the exact moment you were in a sealed London Eye pod and surrounded by witnesses."

"That makes no sense," Oxnard seethed. "How would he know where to come? No one knew I was going to be there. No one knew I'd even *bought* a new yacht until I told Kamran here."

There was the tiniest edge of panic in his voice now, Zaf thought. All week long, these wealthy men had spoken with such confidence, as if they were used to the world bending to their will. It was oddly disturbing to hear something like fear come from one of them.

"You gave the details of the yacht's location on the last post-card you sent him," said Diana. "Oh, you were careful enough to not sign any of them. You probably disguised your hand-writing too, but the pieces add together. You invited him to the yacht so you could kill him and have done with him."

"Di," said Errol, "you might have skipped a page or two there. You just said that Oxnard here invited this Monroth guy to the boat to kill him, but you also said that Oxnard was with us. Which was it?"

"Both," said Diana. "And that was the truly clever part. I've been on the *Silver Salmon* yacht."

"What?" said Oxnard.

"Twice now, actually. You've got some nice art. A lovely Bazille painting."

Zaf, pleased that she'd remembered, nodded at her.

"There's also a statue of a dog in the lounge area. About this high. It's very charming, in a slightly cold way."

"What in the blue blazes are you on about?" said Oxnard.

"A dog," Diana repeated. "Vernon Monroth had a pet dog, a perfectly charming little lad by the name of Turner. Some of us, many of us, just can't resist patting a dog when we meet one."

"I'm really lost now," said Ariadne. "There's a dog."

Diana nodded. "A dog which, when this button is pressed" – she gestured at the device in the bag held by DCI Sugarbrook

– "becomes what I suppose you might call a massive taser. It's capable of delivering a huge electric shock to anyone who touches it. A shock powerful enough to stop a man's heart. Powerful enough to throw a man back two or three steps, out through an open door and over the side of a boat."

"Incredible," said Kamran.

"The statue has been collected by police forensic analysts," said Sugarbrook. "Tests will be conducted."

"A murder with a perfect alibi," said Diana. "Because how could someone commit murder when they are hundreds of feet in the air on the London Eye? It does, of course, offer a perfect vantage point from which to see the yacht so that the device can be activated – and deactivated – at the right moment. It wouldn't do any good to have the killer statue live when a crew member might accidentally touch it."

"I don't know what dog you're talking about!" cried Oxnard. "And I never used that little doohickey you're waving about there."

"It fell from under your napkin at dinner the other night," said Diana. "I saw."

"And I told you then that it wasn't mine!"

"We will test it for fingerprints," said Sugarbrook.

"I might have touched it when she tried to foist it upon me. It's all a trick."

"Oxnard..." said Kamran. "If any of this is true, you should speak honestly."

"It's all lies, dash it, man!" Oxnard fumed. "I've not seen Monroth in years. I dismissed him from my service after... I mean I decided that..."

"After what, mate?" said Errol. He'd placed his hands on the table and was leaning towards Oxnard. "Did you know what happened to Tristram?"

Oxnard looked ashen. The panic in his voice was winning the battle over his arrogant self-belief. Zaf realised that Alexsei was gripping his hand. He gripped back.

Oxnard gulped. "If there's any truth in what this woman says Monroth might have done at the freeport, none of it has anything to do with me. I wouldn't tell him to..." He swallowed, as if the collar of his suit was too tight. "Tristram was our friend, damn it!"

"My God," whispered Kamran. "It's true?"

"Mr Pike," said Sugarbrook, "I think it best that you come to the station to discuss some details with us."

"No, no! It didn't happen! I didn't do it!"

"Sir," said Sugarbrook, "I'd rather not arrest you at this stage, but I will do if you intend to cause a scene. There's a car waiting downstairs and it's only a short drive to Kensington nick."

Oxnard, his eyes bulging, stood, glared at each person one last time, and stormed from the room, followed by DS Quigley.

"I will be sending officers to get statements from the rest of you," said Sugarbrook. "Apologies for disturbing your evening."

And with that, he left.

The departure of Oxnard and the police had seemed to suck the very air from the room. No one spoke for a long time.

Errol was shaking his head and breathing in and out through his nose as though trying to expel the unpleasantness of the situation.

"So, is it true?" said Kamran.

"It's a police matter now," replied Robin.

Diplomatic answer, thought Zaf.

"And I was bloody well looking forward to this week as well," spat Errol.

Alexsei looked at Zaf. "Perhaps we should give them some space," he muttered.

As one, Alexsei, Zaf, Diana and Ariadne made their way out.

"Diana," said Errol, as she crossed to the door.

She turned to him. "Yes, Mr van Blerk."

He stared at her. There was raw, unhappy emotion behind his eyes.

"I suppose I should thank you for bringing this all to our attention," he said.

She nodded.

"And I never want to see your face again," he added. "You understand me?"

CHAPTER SIXTY

"You always were the one to steal the limelight, weren't you?" said Ariadne as the three helpers and Diana left through the Serenity Haven spa, past the new 'shoe art' installation.

"Not my intention, honestly, Ariadne."

Ariadne put her hands on the shoulders of Zaf and Alexsei in front of her. "Oh, this woman! The things I could tell you about our days in showbusiness. The things she would do to make sure the audience's eyes were on her."

Diana was sure Ariadne would have said more, but she was distracted by the sight of the two police cars on the street outside, blue lights silently twirling.

Sugarbrook stood beside one of the vehicles. He lifted his head, a signal to Diana that he wanted to speak to her.

"Anyway," said Ariadne loudly, "Errol van Blerk has offered me a month-long stay at his new hotel in Abu Dhabi or somewhere. Every cloud, et cetera. Gentlemen, it's been a pleasure."

With that as her farewell, she turned north to follow the road in the direction of Baker Street.

"I had best go speak to the detective," said Diana.

"Want us around?" asked Zaf.

Diana shook her head. "It's Friday night. Your weekend starts here."

Alexsei leaned in towards Zaf's shoulder. "Maybe we can sneak out and relax a bit now? My father will not want to speak until morning."

"He's right, Zaf. You go and have fun." Diana crossed to DCI Sugarbrook just as one of the police cars set off.

"How nice that you've landed me with a mountain of work on a Friday evening," said Sugarbrook with a wry smile.

"I hope I haven't contaminated evidence or anything with my – what was it? – sticking my nose in."

"It'll be fine. Of course, you've caused me an entirely different headache."

"Oh?"

"You left me holding that little dog."

She smiled. "Yes, I did."

"And there's no kennels at my station, so he's currently sat in an empty office. And then the pet rescue place isn't open until tomorrow morning."

"I see."

"Which means I'll end up taking him home. And then what's going to happen?"

"I've no idea, Detective."

"My girls are going to fall completely in love with him, aren't they?" He gave her a pretend scowl. "Just what I need in my life – another mouth to feed."

"I'm sure you'll find a solution." Diana turned to make her own way home.

It had been a little while since she had spent a night in her flat in Eccleston Square. Errol van Blerk's luxury spa had been a fun indulgence, but she was glad to return to her home and a familiar bed.

As she settled down in her bed, her phone buzzed with a message from Zaf.

Meet me at the London Eye at 11 tomorrow.

She typed, frowning. *Why?*

Because you didn't get to enjoy it properly the last time we were there.

Diana really didn't need another trip on the London Eye. But Zaf was being kind.

I'll see you there, she responded.

In the morning, Diana rose early and went for her customary walk around the square. So many of the properties here were empty. They were owned by corporations or by wealthy oligarch types not unlike Errol, Kamran and Oxnard. They stood empty and tenantless and if Diana could bring a little joy by tending to some of the plants in their tiny front yards, then she would.

She knew Zaf would be asleep in his own bed on the floor above, but saw no sign of him. Weekend mornings and Zaf were two things that never mixed.

At ten thirty she set out for the London Eye. She walked straight towards the Thames, crossing Vauxhall Bridge by the monstrous MI6 building on the south bank. This route allowed her a delightful view of the Palace of Westminster, which was a biscuity golden colour in the bright morning sun.

She entered the area in front of County Hall, passing among tourists on her way to the wheel that dominated this side of the river.

Someone called her name and she turned.

"Diana, it is you," said Robin Silversmith, coming through the crowd.

"Oh, hello. This is a surprise."

Robin had changed out of her efficient workwear into a tailored tweed jacket over a simple white blouse. Coupled with knee-length boots, she looked like she could be on her way to a gymkhana.

"Your colleague asked me to join you this morning," she said.

"Oh. Has he invited everyone for a fresh turn on the London Eye?"

"I thought he had some questions he wanted to ask. I didn't want to leave anyone with negative lingering impressions from the week."

"It *was* a most unusual week."

"More than is normal," said Robin, smiling. "I gather Mr Pike has already been released on bail. But my sources suggest he will be charged with Mr Monroth's murder before the end of next week."

"There you are!" said Zaf, hurrying towards them with a bunch of tickets in his hand.

"Three of us for this trip?" said Diana.

"Three authentic tickets. Just three. I'm not made of money, you know. Come on."

CHAPTER SIXTY-ONE

DIANA LET Zaf lead them to the queue and soon enough they were in a glass pod with a dozen other tourists, slowly rising into the air.

"I can do my tour guide spiel again if you like," said Zaf, "although it might be a bit similar to the one I gave the first time we were here."

Sun slanted over the buildings in South London, cutting through the pod and warming their backs. Without the air conditioning in these sealed units, Diana could imagine they'd get unbearably hot in the summer.

"Did you know I studied Art History at university?" said Zaf, seemingly out of nowhere.

"Is that so?" replied Robin.

"Never graduated, mind," he said. "But I know art."

"What prompted you to mention that?" said Robin. "The spectacular view?"

He shook his head. Diana wondered if this was going somewhere.

"Just thinking about old Monroth and Oxnard," he said.

"The fake paintings that they passed off as real to bolster Oxnard's fortunes, or which only existed as forged documents."

"There are plenty of rich people whose fortunes were created out of nothing but hot air and bluster," said Robin.

"Right. Fake it till you make it."

"I think I'm more a fan of old-fashioned hard work."

"Hear, hear," said Diana. They were halfway up now, the river receding below them. Diana tried not to think about what she'd seen the last time she was here.

"Of course," said Zaf, "when you come across a fake work of art, one of the things that singles it out as a fake is that it is too much like the original."

Robin frowned. "Too much like the original?"

"Like, um, fanfic. You know, like when people on the internet write Harry Potter fan fiction or Sherlock fan fiction, one of the things that marks it out as a copy of the writer's original is that it leans too heavily into the tics of the original artist."

"Ah," said Robin. "The faker tries too hard to make it appear real."

"Whether it's intended to deceive or not. Exactly. It was bothering me last night."

"Bothering you?"

"How nice it must be to be bothered by the details of fine art," said Diana. "Most young people have more mundane worries."

Over to the east, St Paul's Cathedral was clearly visible. In its shadow was the building that housed the Guild of Tourism, invisible from here. Diana was reminded that she needed to sign Zaf up for his certification.

"No, you see," said Zaf, turning from the view to look at the two women. "Something didn't strike me as right yesterday."

"What was that?" asked Robin.

"The postcards."

Diana watched his face. *What is this about, Zaf?*

"The postcards Mr Pike sent to Monroth?" Robin said.

Zaf nodded, his gaze on Robin's face. "We only got to see half the conversation. We saw Oxnard's postcards to Monroth, but we didn't see any of Monroth's communications to Oxnard."

A shrug. "Maybe the police will turn them up."

"And the last postcard from Monroth's blackmail victim to Monroth invited him to meet on Oxnard's yacht while we were all here. And I said to Diana here that if the meeting was on the yacht, then it seemed obvious the message was from Oxnard."

"Most obvious indeed."

Zaf's eyes widened. He pointed to Diana. "And that's what you said in reply. Those exact words. 'Most obvious indeed'."

"Although where else was Oxnard going to lure him to?" said Diana. "He'd installed the killer dog in the yacht, a place Vernon could be invited to which was both publicly accessible but at the same time private."

"But the very nature of the postcards was..." Zaf screwed up his face. "Oxnard's messages were sent to Monroth on post-cards. But not just any postcards. Distinctive vintage postcards which he'd bought in bulk from a shop we happened to visit this week. Talk about unlucky for Oxnard."

"The rich and the clever both over-estimate the brilliance of their own actions," said Robin. "There's an arrogance that comes from a certain type of person."

"True," said Zaf. "And I'll bet that the police, when they track down the artist who made that dog statue, will find a paper trail of some sort leading back to Oxnard again."

"Arrogance," said Robin again.

Zaf nodded solemnly. "The postcards, the statue, the electronic blipper that turns it on and off, that he was careless enough to leave on the dinner table the other night."

Diana felt the skin on her arms tingle. "Do you think Oxnard might not have committed the crime?"

"He admitted to it last night," said Robin.

"He all but confessed to killing Tristram," said Zaf, "or, to be precise, to knowing that Vernon Monroth had killed Tristram and Oxnard had kept the man's secret. He was a wrong 'un. I bet they'll discover some absolutely stunning lies when the investigators get round to looking at Oxnard's collections." He chuckled grimly. "If Vernon Monroth hadn't died on Oxnard's yacht, no one would have thought to revisit Tristram Ramsgate's death."

"Justice will be served, at last," said Diana.

Zaf eyed her. "I've had a certain piece of art going round and round in my head," he said. "Well, two. There's the *Landscape with Two Figures* by Renoir that I think Monroth was going to try to pass off being in Oxnard's collection or something. Or at least, the half of it that hadn't been recovered. We only know there's two halves because they both appear as one in this painting by Bazille."

"I don't know Bazille," said Robin.

"French impressionist."

"Liked painting *en plein air*," added Diana.

"Which is posh French for doing it outside in public," said Zaf.

"And this painting has been going round in your head?" said Robin.

"It has. It's a painting within a painting. There's the two figures, half the painting now lost to us. Just two people. And then there's this other painting, *Bazille's Studio*, which has a painting of that painting within it but also shows the rest of the room with people in it."

"And it's an especially good painting, is it?" said Robin.

"I don't know. It's more what it means or what thoughts it sparks in my mind. You see, it's a bit like Monroth and Oxnard."

"How so?"

"We have a story with two figures. Monroth and Oxnard. It's a story told in postcard communications, but like the other half of the painting, Monroth's communications to Oxnard are missing. We have only half the picture, half the story."

"Your friend is fond of analogies," Robin said Diana.

Diana raised an eyebrow. The pod was ascending, the Thames receding beneath their feet. She resisted a shiver as she watched Zaf. "I've rarely heard him talk so passionately," she said.

"I've not even got started yet," said Zaf, "because I suspect that, like the other half of the painting, Monroth's communications to Oxnard don't exist."

"I'm sorry... they what?" said Robin.

"Don't exist," said Zaf. "Those postcards, those *very obvious* postcards tell us all the story we need to know. They tell us of demands and shared guilt and a need to meet up. Every one of us who has read them has been able to fill in the gaps. The originals and the replies from Monroth don't need to exist. And I don't think they ever existed."

"I'm sorry," said Robin. "I'm not quite following you. How could they possibly not exist?"

Zaf took a deep breath. Diana sensed nervousness in him.

"It's a fake," he said. "I think it's a fake."

"What's a fake?" said Diana.

"The crime we've been investigating all week. It's a fake."

"A man is dead," Robin reminded him.

"Yes. And he was very obviously murdered. But I don't think Oxnard did it."

"We've just very much established he did."

"It's too obvious. The postcards which can be traced directly to Oxnard's home. The killer remote device which, if I understand it correctly, Diana saw dropped by Oxnard's side at dinner. The fact that Vernon Monroth died on Oxnard's yacht, of all places. Too obvious. Yeah, I can't deny that Oxnard was halfway to confessing that he knew about Tristram's death before the police took him away, but killing Vernon...?"

Diana watched Zaf's face as he spoke. She hadn't thought of this but... he had something.

"It's like the hearse Oxnard used in the race," he said.

"What is?" said Diana.

"Death. It draws attention. It draws a reaction. If someone knew that Oxnard had a hand in Tristram's death and if someone wanted both Monroth and Oxnard to get their just desserts, then killing Monroth would be a decent way of getting the police's attention." He looked at Robin. "You must have thought your plan had gone horribly wrong when Monroth fell off the side of the yacht."

Robin gave a light cough of surprise. "My plan?"

Zaf nodded. "Your plan."

CHAPTER SIXTY-TWO

ROBIN GAZED BACK AT ZAF, saying nothing. They were at the apex of the wheel's circumference, pods on both sides and sky above.

"How did you discover that Monroth had killed Tristram?" asked Zaf.

Robin remained silent.

"It could have been something simple," Zaf said. "A man like Monroth, poor and bitter, maybe he said something to someone in a local pub. A brag. Maybe that got back to you. Even if you heard that, there wasn't any physical evidence to tie him and Oxnard to Tristram's death. It was years ago. So... you plotted your revenge."

"We will do anything to honour the ones we love," said Diana.

"Love is a powerful motivator," agreed Zaf. "And you did love Tristram."

Robin's eyes flashed.

"Employer, employee," said Diana. "But that mutual

respect. That was a love as meaningful as any. And Tristram should not have died as he died."

Robin stared at Zaf. She said nothing.

"So, you made your plans," said Zaf. "You had time to prepare. You knew Monroth had a dog. You concocted that wild murder method. Maybe you got the person who made the bodycams to rig the statue up to give an electric shock. You made a batch order of postcards to be sent to Oxnard's address while, I guess, buying individual ones anonymously so you could send them to Monroth."

Diana nodded. He was right. She'd been wrong, and Zaf had spotted it.

"You installed the statue on the *Silver Salmon* yacht," she said to Robin. "I think we've all seen that Oxnard doesn't even know half the art he owns."

Zaf continued. "You wanted the world to believe Oxnard had set up a piece of fake art with an ulterior purpose, like the shoe exhibit Newton's put in the spa. And then when Monroth came to the yacht, you observed from up here," said Zaf, "and turned the device on at the critical moment, and then off again."

"You placed the remote under Oxnard's napkin at the table," said Diana. "Hoping or planning that he would take it or, as was the case, someone else would see him with it. All very risky."

Robin's head moved ever so slightly.

Something tugged at the hem of Diana's jacket. Behind her on the central bench of the pod was an elderly woman. The woman's hand, resting on top of a walking stick, waggled at the three of them.

"Excuse, me. Is this all a show? A bit of play acting?"

Robin smiled. "Yes. It's all pretend."

"It's proper good," said the woman. "You're all very convincing."

"Very convincing," agreed Robin. "None of it is true or real."

Zaf made a noise in his throat. "Well, there is one thing. It's really minor."

"Yes?" said Robin.

"Yesterday, when Oxnard was protesting his innocence, he unhelpfully pointed out that none of you had seen his yacht before, that no one even knew he'd bought a new yacht. He thought that would show Monroth couldn't have known where to go, but it was actually more incriminating."

"Yes," said Robin.

"It's a Starchaser yacht."

"It is."

"And you happened to mention that fact before we even saw it come along the river."

Robin frowned, her eyebrow twitching. "Did I?"

"You did."

"And," Diana added, "when I brought Vernon's dog into the spa, I think you recognised him. You were momentarily lost for words."

"Was I?"

"You were. Perhaps during the course of your preparations, you spent a lot of time by Vernon's houseboat, spying on him." She paused, rethought. "Or perhaps it was more intricate than that. Those postcards we found at the houseboat. They were not hard to find. Maybe you met the dog while you were arranging that scene. Or..." She chuckled grimly. "Maybe the only postcards Vernon had ever received were the ones I'd seen him with at the London Eye. Perhaps they were a simple request to meet, a promise of financial rehabilitation with none of the bewildering responses to Vernon's entirely fictitious blackmailing attempt."

Zaf nodded in eager agreement. "So the ones at the houseboat were just window-dressing."

Robin gripped the handrail running along the curved windows of their pod.

"Does it really matter how I did it? Justice *has* been served, hasn't it?" she said.

"A kind of justice," said Diana.

"We could forget about all of this and get on with our lives."

Zaf grimaced and pointed down. Diana and Robin both looked to where he was pointing. Among the crowds on the south bank was a cluster of hi-vis vests and, among them, an ant-like figure that might well be the hulking form of DCI Clint Sugarbrook.

Robin let out a sigh. Part relief, part exasperation.

"I suppose I should thank you, Diana."

"Thank me?" said Diana.

"I hadn't envisaged him dying anywhere but on that boat at the very scene of the crime. Dead, beside the statue that had killed him, a wealth of subtle clues – but not *too* subtle – pointing at Oxnard Pike as his accomplice and his killer. If you hadn't seen him fall, if you hadn't decided to investigate..."

"Never underestimate the dogged determination of a woman of a certain age," said Diana. "And if it's any consolation, I didn't suspect you for an instant. You have a killer poker face."

"I don't regret anything I've done," said Robin. "The truth will come out now. That's all I wanted."

Diana reached out and gripped Zaf's arm, impressed by his unpicking of this final mystery.

Robin looked down through the glass, at the police waiting for her. The pod descended, its other occupants silent.

"If you'll permit me," said Robin, "I'll enjoy the view while I still have the chance."

Hands on the rail, she gazed out over London. Bright sunshine picked out the details of the nearest buildings and cast its glow over the entire city. It was going to be a fine day.

READ A FREE STORY, GUS THE THEATRE CAT

Gus the tabby cat is now a firm fixture at Chartwell and Crouch Bus Tours. Newton the bus driver has taken him under his wing and regularly provides him with cans of tuna. And the tour guides Diana and Zaf are finding he's a hit with the guests.

But then when Diana and Zaf are showing a group of theatre professionals around London, Gus disappears in a West End theatre.

Newton is distraught. He's searched the theatre high and low but can't find his beloved feline friend.

One night, when Diana and Zaf are watching the performance, he has a plan. It involves plenty of cunning, a fair amount of sneaking around in the auditorium and quite a lot of tinned tuna.

Can Newton find Gus without causing total chaos for the audience?

Find out in this London Cozy Mysteries short story.

Read *Gus the Theatre Cat* for FREE at rachelmclean. com/gus.

READ THE LONDON COSY MYSTERIES SERIES

Death at Westminster

Death in the West End

Death at Tower Bridge

Death on the Thames

...and more to come

Buy from book retailers or via the Rachel McLean website.

ALSO BY RACHEL MCLEAN

The McBride & Tanner Series – Buy from book retailers or via the Rachel McLean website.

Blood and Money

Death and Poetry

Power and Treachery

...and more to come

The Cumbria Crime Series by Rachel McLean and Joel Hames – Buy from book retailers or via the Rachel McLean website.

The Harbour

The Mine

The Cairn

...and more to come

ALSO BY MILLIE RAVENSWORTH

The Cozy Craft Mysteries – Buy now in ebook and paperback

The Wonderland Murders

The Painted Lobster Murders

The Sequinned Cape Murders

The Swan Dress Murders

The Tie-Dyed Kaftan Murders

The Scarecrow Murders